NO SHO...

Stillman lunged for the ... as he brought his Colt to bear, grabbing the gun aimed at his belly just as Free pulled the trigger. As if in slow motion, Stillman and Free watched the hammer start toward the firing pin. Stillman's stomach muscles clenched as he awaited the imminent bark and bullet . . . but nothing happened.

He looked down and saw why. His hand had dropped over the gun so that the webbing between thumb and index finger had intercepted the hammer about a quarter of an inch before it hit the firing pin.

Both men froze in their positions, staring at Stillman's hand pinned to the gun by the hammer. Then Free lifted his shocked eyes to Stillman's.

His heart starting to beat again, Stillman grinned at the man, grabbed the gun away, and swung the butt of his Henry rifle against Free's skull, laying him out cold.

10   202 1

Praise for Peter Brandvold:

"Takes off like a shot, never giving the reader a chance to set the book down."
—Douglas Hirt

"A writer to watch."
—Jory Sherman

Titles by Peter Brandvold

ONCE HELL FREEZES OVER
ONCE A LAWMAN
ONCE MORE WITH A .44
BLOOD MOUNTAIN
ONCE A MARSHAL

ONCE HELL FREEZES OVER

PETER BRANDVOLD

BERKLEY BOOKS, NEW YORK

ONCE HELL FREEZES OVER

A Berkley Book / published by arrangement with
the author

PRINTING HISTORY
Berkley edition / October 2001

ISBN: 0-425-17248-1

BERKLEY®
Berkley Books are published by The Berkley Publishing Group,
a division of Penguin Putnam Inc.,
375 Hudson Street, New York, New York 10014.
BERKLEY and the "B" design
are trademarks belonging to Penguin Putnam Inc.

PRINTED IN THE UNITED STATES OF AMERICA

10 9 8 7 6 5 4 3 2 1

For *mi amigo*, Brad Thorson

Happy is the home that shelters a friend.

—Emerson

1

ESCORTING THE ARMY paymaster through the wilds of Montana always gave Corporal Gordon C. McGuane the willies. Thieves were always a threat to the cash stashed in Sergeant Hollis Trumbull's saddle-bags, but today McGuane was feeling especially off his feed, the hair on the back of his neck standing straight up in the air.

He rode his Army gelding ahead of the six-man detail with a keen eye on the mail road ahead, and on the shaggy, snow-dusted slopes closing around them. A day and a half out of Fort Assiniboine, and packing fifty thousand dollars in Army payroll money, the detail was climbing into the southern reaches of the Two Bear Mountains, heading southeast toward the Army outpost at Lewistown, on the other side of the Missouri River.

In the day and a half they'd been riding, McGuane and the others had seen nothing out of the ordinary. They'd seen the usual hawks, coyotes, gophers—thousands of gophers, especially down on the prairie—and they'd even spotted a grizzly through Private Tate's field glasses. The grizzly had been moving away toward a river cut, in its characteristic lumbering amble, and not a threat. The Indians they'd seen yesterday weren't a threat, either—a ragtag group of down-at-the-heels Chippewa and Cree, mostly children and old people, heading for Fort Assiniboine and a place to camp.

No, nothing out of the ordinary. McGuane had seen no sun reflection off a rifle barrel or spur, no distant dust plume, no sign of movement on one of the rocky ledges jutting out of the winter-tawny mountain above them . . . no sign of anything threatening whatsoever. By all appearances, McGuane and the others were alone out here, and relatively safe.

That was why McGuane's unease would have been as perplexing to the others, had they been aware of it, as it was to him. All he knew was that near him now were plenty of boulders and bramble patches where would-be bushwackers could effect an ambush, and a cold fear tickled the back of McGuane's neck as he pondered the possibility.

He'd be happy when they got to the outpost at Lewistown and were rid of the money once and for all. McGuane thought he'd even look into being relieved of his paymaster duties. Hell, he'd rather cut wood and haul it out of the mountains than ride shotgun for old Trumbull. The corporal's imagination was just too keen . . . had been all his life.

The men behind McGuane talked as they rode, laughing with the gabby paymaster about a farm widow named Margaret who apparently gave Trumbull shelter one cold winter's night, and a whole lot more.

"Boys, that woman worked me over so good, I could hardly crawl up on my horse the next day!" The red-faced sergeant slapped his thigh and wheezed with laughter.

McGuane wanted them all to be quiet, but Sergeant

Trumbull was in charge. If McGuane said anything they'd think he was just being skittish, an old woman trying to put a damper on their fun.

They'd ridden for another half hour when McGuane reined his horse off the trail. The men had taken a nature stop an hour ago, but he'd been too nervous to do likewise. He'd stayed mounted and kept lookout from a spur. Now, however, the Army hardtack had gotten the better of him.

"You men go ahead," he said. "I've got personal business."

As McGuane dismounted, one man laughed. Another said, "Go to it, Corporal."

Trumbull said, "It's your nerves that got you so damn irregular, Gordon. You have to learn to lighten up a little."

The last man swung around in his saddle to smile back at McGuane. "You want Jimmy Boy here to stay behind and wipe your ass for you, Corp? He'd be more than happy to."

"Ah, shut up, Decker," Jimmy Boy said as the column drifted out of hearing. "You're the one always wants to play grabby-pants every Satu'dee night."

Then they disappeared around a stand of mountain firs. Corporal McGuane tied his horse to a branch, and headed through the spare forest covering the hillside, looking for a log.

When he found one, he removed his gun and cartridge belt, dropped his trousers, and settled down to business. He wished he would have done it earlier; now he seemed to have constipated himself. It being only about thirty degrees, it was too damn cold to sit out here long with your privates exposed.

The unease McGuane had been experiencing dragged out his constitutional even longer than its postponement had done. When he finally finished, he retrieved a couple of fallen leaves and some sticks with which to wipe himself. Then, with an owlish grunt, looking warily around, he pulled his pants back up and strapped his gun and cartridge belt around his waist.

When he'd gotten back on his horse and headed down the trail, he felt considerably lighter—both physically and mentally. Maybe a good constitutional was all he really needed, he mused. But then he saw the column down the grade to his right.

They had stopped, and before them stood two men in wool coats and Stetsons. One of the men was half-carrying the other, his friend's arm draped over his shoulder as if injured.

McGuane halted his horse, his pulse quickening, the old feeling of unease returning with a vengeance. Something was wrong. He could sense it.

He looked around at the ridges shouldering above each side of the trail. He was bringing his eyes back down when he saw something flash in a bramble patch.

"Hey!" McGuane yelled, giving his horse the spurs and plunging down the bank.

He unsnapped the cover over his Army-issue revolver, and drew the pistol. He yelled again. Three soldiers looked back at him annoyed. The paymaster and Private Jimmy Donleavy had dismounted and were talking to the injured man and his friend, who now looked toward McGuane, barreling toward them on his horse.

McGuane gestured wildly with his arm. "It's a trap, goddamnit!" he yelled. "It's a trap . . . *get the hell out of there!*"

All the soldiers turned to him looking skeptical and annoyed. "What the hell is he yelling about now?" they seemed to say. None of them saw the revolvers the injured man and his friend produced from their mackinaws. One man pointed his gun at Trumbull's back, the other at Donleavy's. The soldiers jerked forward an instant before the two staccato pistol shots reached McGuane's ears. A second later both the sergeant and Jimmy Donleavy stumbled forward, falling.

"*No!*" McGuane cried, aiming his pistol. But the other soldiers were between him and the two farmers, so drawing a decent bead was impossible.

The other soldiers, slow to react, were turning around now to the source of the gunfire. Awkwardly, confused, they drew their own side arms, but before they could level them, smoke puffed from the tree- and rock-covered slopes on either side of them. Ear-piercing rifle fire exploded all at once, like two bombs on a timed detonator placed on both sides of the trail.

The harsh reports echoed in the narrow canyon, the slugs tearing through the mounted soldiers, spitting blood from their wool coats. Their screaming mounts crow-hopped, sunfished, and bucked, throwing the wounded soldiers to the stone-hard ground, where they cursed and cried and stumbled to their feet, only to be cut down again by the cross fire.

One of the men—hatless, face and neck bloody—ran back toward McGuane screaming. He'd run only about fifteen feet when one of the bushwackers stepped casually onto the trail behind him, lifted his pistol, and fired. The private's head sprouted blood. His knees gave, and he stumbled and fell back on his heels.

McGuane's horse jumped the dying man. Screaming for all he was worth, too outraged now to consider falling back and going for help, McGuane lowered his pistol and fired at the gunman.

His shot missed. The gunman's return bullet did not. McGuane felt the slug hit him in the chest like a sledge-hammer. It turned him just enough that he could see the rifle on the south-facing slope turn his way. As if in agonizing slowness, the barrel sprouted smoke and flames.

McGuane rolled backward off his buck-kicking mount. He hit the ground on his chest, groaning and spitting blood and trying desperately to claw his way to his knees. His horse trampled him as the beast turned from the gunfire and headed back the way it had come. McGuane was pounded by the flailing hooves, and then thrown sideways.

He lay there looking up at the cold blue sky, feeling blood leak from his wounds. He was going numb. He thought vaguely about his gun, but knew trying for it was no use. He couldn't move.

Then a big cloud covered the sky. McGuane blinked to clear his vision.

It wasn't a cloud. It was the big dark face of a grizzled man in a flat-brimmed hat looking down at him. The man grinned, showing one silver front tooth, and brought his pistol to bear on McGuane's head.

The silver tooth was the last thing Corporal McGuane saw.

"See ya in hell, soldier boy," were the last words he heard.

2

FAY STILLMAN BROUGHT her black mare up out of the draw and mounted the grassy ridge at a gallop, her black hair bouncing on the shoulders of her heavy wool poncho, and the folds of her slitted riding skirt slapping against her thighs. When she'd made the ridge top, she could tell by the black mare's wide eyes and frisky snorts that the animal was not yet in need of a rest. The animal would, in fact, take it as a personal insult if Fay tried to rein her in.

"Okay, Dorothy—have it your way!" Fay cried as she and the horse descended the ridge's other side, plummeting down through the dead winter grass and scattered, spindly chokecherry shrubs.

For the past few weeks, there had been too much snow on the ground for a decent ride, but this week's chinook winds had blown it off, leaving only crusty gray patches here and there on the leeward sides of hills. All around Fay stretched the vast, brown, empty plain, dipping and pitching as it rose steadily toward the foothills of the Two Bear Mountains, south of Clantick, Montana Territory. Riding with the wind in her hair, adrenaline

pumping in her veins, the cool breeze numbing her
cheeks, and Dorothy's heavy snorts in her ears, Fay felt
a keen exhilaration.

The world streaked past at a gallop, and Fay's cares
were a million miles away. She knew Dorothy felt it,
too, for the poor animal, so used to Fay's Saturday rides
in the mountains, had been cooped up in the pasture
behind the buggy shed.

"Go, girl! Go, Dorothy! That's it. . . ."

Finally, a mile farther on, they ascended a swale and
pulled up on the two-track wagon road, Fay easing back
on Dorothy's reins. "Ooo-kay . . . I think we've had
enough for now, girl," she said. "Don't want you all
lathered up when we get to the Hawley place, or you'll
catch cold."

The black snorted, breathing hard, and pricked her
ears, rolling her eyes around hungrily. Fay knew the
mare had another hard mile in her, but they were too
close to the Hawley farm to keep galloping. So Fay
aimed Dorothy southward along the trail, gave her some
head, but held her to a trot.

Fay took the trail, which branched off down a coulee,
and followed it to the top of a hill overlooking the Hawley farm. She reined Dorothy to a stop under a lone box
elder and appraised the farmstead below—the one-and-
a-half-story log house issuing smoke through its stone
chimney, the jerry-built barn and shed, and the windmill
standing at the center of it all, a wood stock tank at its
feet. There was a haphazard air about the place, the
house and barn needing new shingles and fresh chinking
between the logs. A pile of corral poles lay in the high
weeds around the outbuildings, scattered like jackstraws.

Still, the place looked better than when Fay had last
seen it, when she and Crystal Harmon had come over a
few months ago and locked Earl Hawley in his barn. It

was Crystal's alcohol "cure," and it seemed to have worked, for most of the tools and discarded harness had been picked up around the grounds, the wheeled gear moved into the barn and sheds. There hadn't been time to do much more, since it was winter, but Fay was hopeful the house would be reshingled come spring, flowers would be planted around the foundation, and the garden would be worked.

From everything Fay had heard and now seen, she was convinced Earl Hawley was well on his way to a full recovery from his bout with the bottle. One thing she knew for sure was that his young daughter, Candace, was attending school, for Fay was the girl's teacher. When Earl had been drinking, he'd made Candace stay home and work on the farm, which was what had motivated Fay and Crystal to initiate the "cure" in the first place.

Smiling bemusedly at the progress that seemed to have been made here, Fay touched Dorothy with her spurs and descended the hill to the farmyard, where a black and white dog ran out from under the porch to greet her, barking and wagging its tail. The house door opened and eleven-year-old Candace appeared, wearing a poke bonnet and a long, full gingham skirt trimmed with ribbon and large bows.

"Mrs. Stillman!" she waved.

"Well, look at you!"

The dark-haired child flushed shyly and fingered the dress's hem. "Momma made it for me special."

"Oh, Candace—it's lovely! Happy birthday, child."

The door opened wider and Fay watched Earl Hawley step out from behind his daughter. Hawley was a big, broad-shouldered, ham-handed man with jug ears and thin dark hair combed straight back from his forehead. He was wearing a suit coat a size too small, and a string tie that looked a little frayed, but it was apparent the man was doing all he could to look his best today, his daughter's eleventh birthday.

"Hello, Mrs. Stillman," he said, coming down the steps. "I'll take your horse for you."

"Why, thank you, Earl. I'd appreciate that," Fay said, dismounting, feeling uncomfortable in the presence of the man she and Crystal had knocked out cold in his own kitchen, then dragged off to a stable in his own barn. She wouldn't have been a bit surprised if Earl harbored more than a little resentment for the attack.

"I'll give her some oats and a rubdown. Looks like you been gallopin'."

"Yes, I gave the girl her head today. She's been cooped up in the pasture for the past three weeks."

Earl took the reins from Fay, smiling wistfully. "I don't mean to be snoopy or nothin', Mrs. Stillman . . . but do you ever ride in a buggy?"

Fay laughed and shook her rich dark hair out from the collar of her poncho. "Earl, you sound like my husband!"

"Well . . . you bein' a sheriff's wife and all. . . ."

"I know, I know—I should try and act the part on occasion."

"No offense, ma'am," Earl said. "You and Crystal . . . you two must be cut from the same cloth, 'cause I don't reckon I ever seen her in a buggy before today."

"Today? I take it she's here, then?"

"She and Jody—they're both here, ma'am. Jody wouldn't let her come alone on account o' her condition an' all." Earl started leading Dorothy toward the barn. "You go right in, Mrs. Stillman." He stopped suddenly and turned to face her. "An' . . . an' I didn't mean no offense by askin' you about the buggy an' all." His face was flushed with embarrassment.

"None taken," Fay said with a laugh, feeling sorry for the poor man, revisited today by the two very same horseback-riding women who'd knocked him out with a two-by-four.

"Come on, Mrs. Stillman," Candace said, taking Fay's hand and leading her up the porch steps. Then, regarding the two brightly wrapped packages that Fay had retrieved from her saddlebags, she asked, "Are those for me?"

"Well, you're the birthday girl, aren't you?"

"Oh, boy! Jody and Crystal brought me presents, too!"

Candace's mother, Mrs. Hawley, stood holding the inside door open. "Fay, thank you so much for coming."

"How could I not come to my favorite student's birthday party?" Fay said, giving the woman a hug. "How are you, Doreen? You look wonderful."

Doreen Hawley flushed and looked down. She wore a crisp gingham dress with lace around the neckline and sleeves, and her hair was held in a shiny bun with an ivory comb. Fay hadn't lied—the woman did look wonderful, so much better than when Fay had first met her, a frightened mouse of a woman held hostage by a brooding, sporadically violent man who drank to dull the sting of life's hardships and disappointments. Now there was hope in Doreen Hawley's large brown eyes, which now more than ever resembled her daughter's.

"Oh, Fay . . . please," she said. "A compliment coming from a lady with your looks is just too much for me to bear."

"How 'bout from one with my looks?" said another voice, dull with sarcasm.

Fay turned to see her best friend, Crystal Harmon, sitting in a rocker by the kitchen wood stove, hands laced over her pregnant belly—about as big a belly as

Fay had ever seen on a young woman Crystal's size. Crystal was wearing a loose-fitting pair of overalls with a checked flannel shirt. Somehow, the honyonker garb did not diminish the twenty-year-old young woman's tomboyish, blue-eyed beauty in the least.

Fay laughed, bringing a hand to her mouth with a mixture of awe and embarrassment. "Crystal! When on earth are you going to deliver that child?"

Crystal rolled her eyes. "I wish I'd do it right now, but then I guess I'd spoil the party."

"If she doesn't do it soon, I'm leavin' until she does," her husband, Jody, said. The tall, darkly handsome young man with half-Cree blood stood beside the kitchen table, a coffee cup steaming up from the oilcloth to his right. He wore a cowhide vest over a cream flannel shirt loosely tied at his sun-darkened neck with rawhide cords. "She's gettin' so owly it's all I can do to keep from tying a rag over her mouth."

"You just try it, bucko, and see how good I am with a bird gun."

"See?" Jody said to Fay.

Candace laughed. Her mother smiled. Crystal's sour moods, the result of her pregnancy, were infamous throughout the mountains—at least, everywhere Jody had spread the word. It was also known that Jody and Crystal Harmon had been in love since they were children playing in the woods and swimming in the creeks of the Two Bear Mountains. They were in love now more than ever, the long-awaited child in Crystal's belly the high point of their lives together. Their back-and-forth chiding had always been part of their lovemaking— long before they'd actually started making love. They ranched five miles southwest of the Hawley farm, on the place Jody's father, Bill Harmon, and his Cree wife had settled nearly twenty years ago.

Laughing, Fay crossed the room to Crystal, kissed her cheek, and patted her belly. "In a few more weeks, you're going to be just as happy as can be." She looked at Jody. "And so will you, Mr. Harmon. How are you, anyway? I haven't seen you in a coon's age."

"Busy as ever, getting ready for calving. How's the sheriff?"

"Ben's fine. At least, he was an hour ago. He and Leon were called out this morning after horse thieves."

"Oh? Whose horses?"

"The Majerus outfit."

Jody frowned. "That's just the other side of the ridge. I hope he catches 'em."

"I'm sure he won't come home until he does," Fay said with a sigh, allowing Mrs. Hawley to take her poncho, hat, and the presents she'd brought for Candace.

"You have a seat at the table," Doreen said, heading for a bedroom off the kitchen. "I'll have dinner on the table in a few minutes."

Fay sat beside Jody, and Candace sat across from them, shuttling her eyes between them and Crystal, as though she had something on her mind. "I learned another poem, Mrs. Stillman."

"Candace—you didn't!"

"Sure enough. I'll recite it for you after dinner, if you want."

"Well, I know I'd like to hear it. How about you two?" Fay asked Jody and Crystal.

"I'd love to hear it, Candace," Crystal said.

Smiling thoughtfully, Jody said, "My pa used to recite poems to me and Ma."

Conspiratorially across the table to Fay, Candace said, "I think this is going to be a really nice birthday—don't you, Mrs. Stillman?"

Unaware of the storm building over the mountains,

and of Adler's men, only eight miles south as the crow flies and headed their way, Fay smiled and grasped the child's hand in hers. "Candace, I'm positively sure of it."

3

STILL GRINNING DOWN at the man he'd just killed, Wayne Adler holstered his pistol. "Too bad, blue-belly," he grumbled, his grin turning to a dark stare.

"Wayne, I got it!" one of his compatriots cried behind him.

Adler turned. The two other men in his band had joined him and the other "farmer," Antoine Riemersma, who held up the paymaster's saddlebags, the trophy they'd all been after.

All four men, including Adler, were rough-looking, hard-edged criminals in tattered trail clothes, battered hats, and heavy coats. The big, shaggy-headed idiot, Benji Phelps, wore a bear coat, which did nothing to make him appear more civilized or more human. Adler had met all three men in the territorial pen at Deer Lodge, and they were bound only by greed and ruthless cunning.

They'd been planning the raid on the paymaster for two months, when the last of them, T. J. Cross, had been released from his cage after promising the parole board he'd no longer be a threat to women and little girls.

Adler cared little for rapists and child molesters, but he allowed the man to ride with him because Cross was good with a .45. Very good. Better than John Wesley Hardin, some said.

Cross, Riemersma, and Benji Phelps were going through the tunics of the dead soldiers, removing valuables. Cross even tipped a dead man's head back to peer into his mouth, looking for gold.

"Come on, you goddamn savages!" Adler yelled, heading for the hill, at the top of which their horses were picketed. "Let's get the hell out of here. You never know who might have been drawn by the gunfire."

"Wait, Wayne," Benji pleaded. The shaggy-headed, baby-faced man in the bear coat was kneeling down next to one of the soldiers. He was pulling on one of the corpse's fingers. "I wanna get this ring off o' this here finger, Wayne!"

"Leave it, Benji—I'll buy you a new one, for God sakes."

"I like this one here, Wayne—its got a big pretty rock in it!"

"Benji!"

Adler, Cross, and Riemersma, who had the paymaster's saddlebags on his shoulder, climbed the hill, pulling at the grass and shrubs for leverage. At the hilltop, studded with ponderosa pines and rock outcroppings, the three men sat down to catch their breath. Riemersma dropped the saddlebags. Adler went through them.

"How much?" Cross asked.

He was a tall, wiry, slope-shouldered hombre with a hawk nose and dumb brown eyes set too close together. His face had been ravaged by smallpox, so that in a certain light it resembled an old coffee can that had been used for target practice. Adler, who had always done fairly well with women—the sporting kind, anyway—

figured it was Cross's ugliness that had forced him to resort to rape.

Adler was still counting the small, neatly packed bundles of greenbacks. "Looks like there must be close to fifty thousand dollars here."

"No shit?" Riemersma said.

Five feet ten and potbellied, he was the oldest of the crew by at least ten years. His curly hair was gray-flecked, his face heavily seamed from all the years he'd spent in prison rock quarries. His nose was broad and bulging with all the times it had been broken and improperly set. But there was a softness in his eyes, a wry sense of humor, that belied the hardened criminal within. His criminality, his penchant for common thievery, was mostly due to sloth rather than belligerence or a home-grown contempt for society, which was Adler's primary stimulus.

Like Cross, Adler just plumb hated life, and he'd discovered meaning in little but a modified, professional hedonism.

"Would I shit you, Tony?"

"Fifty thousand, split four ways is . . ." Riemersma paused to mentally calculate his winnings.

"Twelve thousand five hundred, dumb-ass," Adler said.

He heard someone running hard, and turned to see Benji Phelps climbing the hill, looking like he was about to die from a stroke. His child's fleshy face was bright red, and his unruly mop of curls bounced around his head. But he was grinning.

"Look what I got! Look what I got!" he wheezed as he approached, collapsing on his knees. He brought his meaty right paw up and opened it.

Adler peered at Benji's hand and winced. In the big man's palm was a finger with a ring still attached.

"Oh, Jesus H. Christ, Benji!"

Cross laughed. Riemersma looked away and shook his head.

"Ain't it pretty?" Benji said, like a kid on Christmas morning. He picked up the finger and yanked the ring off. Casting away the finger like annoying refuse, he held the ring up to admire it. "It's big and fat and gold, and its got a big blue rock in it."

"Fool's gold," Riemersma scoffed. "And the rock is glass . . . you idiot."

Benji shrugged, his jubilation over his booty not abated in the least. "Well, it looks nice." He tried to put it on his ring finger. It was like trying to put a delicate diamond wedding band on a ring of baloney. He tried all his fingers. Nothing doing. Finally, he thrust the ring in his coat pocket, shrugged, and said, "I can still look at it."

Adler looked at Riemersma and shook his head. The big, dumb man-child was more interested in a bauble worth no more than five dollars than a saddlebag bulging with Army greenbacks.

"Let's get the horses and get the hell out of here," the square-jawed Adler said.

They found their horses back in the trees, tied to a picket line, and mounted up. Reining northward, they hoped to make Canada in two days, which they thought they could do if they rode hard and no storms pinned them down . . . or posses. The latter was unlikely, since they'd planned the ambush in as remote a place as possible, with little chance of the dead soldiers being discovered for days. But this time of the year—early February—a storm was entirely too possible, especially this far north in Montana.

The thought had no sooner crossed Adler's mind than he saw a snowflake—really more of a grainy ice crystal, but portentous just the same—fall on his horse's mane. Glancing behind him, toward the gnarled cuts and buttes of the Missour River breaks, he cast his gaze southward and felt a heavy dread.

The sky over the undulating hills and mountains had filled with a solid mass of purple clouds, the scalloped edges of which appeared to be moving northward, toward Adler and the others.

Goddamn the luck, anyway.

"What do you say we stop for coffee soon?" Riemersma asked after they'd ridden another half hour. He hadn't seen the clouds.

"Shut up and keep riding," Adler said.

Ride as they did, hard, for the next two hours, they did not get ahead of the fast-building storm. The stray, intermittent ice grains came down harder and harder, soaking the men through their long underwear. Then the wind picked up, like a knife edge slashing their faces. The sleet turned to snow, which quickly covered the shrubs and weeds—a heavy, wet cover that bowed tree limbs, froze mustaches, and made hat brims sag.

Above, the sky grew darker and darker, the ground whiter and whiter, the heavy flakes turning downy and whipped by the wind into drifts. The snow thickened on the men's thighs like woolly chaps. Soon it was as high as their horses' hocks. Peering through it was like trying to take a reckoning through a javelin storm. Trying to stick to a trail was impossible, and it wasn't long before whiteness lay all about them, shunted this way and that by a stern, breath-devouring gale.

Adler knew from the time he'd spent in this country that this was only the beginning of a flagship clipper. They needed to find a stage station or a line shack fast, or they'd all be up to their stirrups in snow. And the way the wind had already numbed his nose, he knew the temperature was going to do nothing but fall.

If they didn't find somewhere to light and dry out fast, they'd all be dead in an hour.

The only problem was, he'd lost the trail they'd been following at least a half hour ago. He wasn't sure, but he suddenly sensed they'd been riding in circles . . . up one canyon, down another, then back up the first.

"What are we gonna do, Wayne?" Riemersma said, his voice nearly lost in the wind and the sandy sound of the snow blowing against their frozen clothes and leather.

Adler had no idea, so he just kept riding, spurring his frightened horse to a trot that gradually fell to a half-hearted, swing-legged walk.

Benji Phelps moaned like a frightened child alone in a dark room. Cross cursed furiously. Riemersma said, "Wayne, we have to get shelter fast," then, five minutes later, "Wayne, we're in some kind of trouble. You know where there's a line shack or somethin' . . . *anything*?"

Adler stopped suddenly, sniffing the air.

"What is it?" Cross asked.

"I think I smell smoke. Wait here."

Adler spurred his tired, frightened horse up a rocky rise, the horse nearly falling twice in the slippery snow, and looked down the other side. Below, through the wind-driven snow opened a broad, bowl-shaped valley, gauzy under the storm, which all but buried it. The gray outlines of a cabin, a barn, several corrals, and outbuildings shone like a tentative sketch on a heavy white canvas. Yellow light shone in the windows of the house like beacons.

Adler sighed and shook his head with relief, then reined his half-dead horse back down the hill. Riemersma asked through gritted teeth, "What'd you find?"

Adler's cold, taut lips cracked a smile. "Shelter, Tony, my boy. Shelter."

4

BEN STILLMAN HALTED his horse and held up a gloved hand for his deputy, Leon McMannigle, to do likewise. Both men sat on the path they'd been following since they'd turned up Moony's Coulee about a mile back, and listened.

The breeze sifted through the pines and a magpie flitted over the trail ahead, tail-heavy and giving its customary shriek. Stillman said, "I thought I heard a horse whinny."

McMannigle sat his gelding wearing a sheepskin coat and black plainsman hat with a low crown and a flat brim. The former buffalo soldier held a Spencer repeater across the bows of his saddle.

"There's a cabin about a half mile ahead," he said to Stillman. "Must've come from there."

"Line shack?"

"Old trapper's cabin. I waited out a storm there once. We could get above it if we climbed that ridge." McMannigle nodded at the pine- and aspen-covered mountain shouldering up on their right.

Stillman scratched his big chin, turning to look up the

high, grassy butte on their left. He was a slim-waisted, broad-shouldered man, a little over six feet tall, with longish salt-and-pepper hair and a bushy salt-and-pepper mustache. He wore a buckskin mackinaw and a big Stetson with the skin of a diamondback wrapped around the crown. The rifle in his hands was a Henry sixteen-shot repeater with a gold-plated, factory-engraved receiver and a pearl bull's head embedded in the smooth walnut stock.

"Any cover over here?" Stillman asked, jerking a thumb at the butte.

It looked like an old volcano, with talus slides and patches of shrubs in its shallow gullies. There was a sprinkling of firs and ponderosa pines on the western slope.

"Just around the bend in the trail, there's an outcropping, about fifty yards up-trail from the cabin," said McMannigle. "What are you thinking?"

"I'm thinking you should take the ridge, and I'll take the outcropping. From the outcropping I should be able to see what's doing at the cabin. When I raise my rifle, you come down the ridge and meet me at the front door."

"You don't think they'll be expecting us?"

Stillman shrugged and gave a wry smile. "I didn't say that."

A light flashed in Leon's mud-black eyes. "I reckon this could get right interestin'. We'd better move fast. Doc said he smelled a storm in the air earlier. If he's right, we sure as hell don't want to be in these mountains when it hits."

Stillman nodded. "Meet you at the cabin."

Leon reined his horse off the trail. Coaxing the gray with hushed commands, he climbed the ridge through the trees, the horse's hooves thudding on the winter-hard ground. Rein chains jangled faintly and the leather squeaked. In a moment, horse and rider had disappeared in the trees up the mountain, and only the snapping of twigs and branches could be heard, growing faint with distance.

Stillman kicked his bay around the bend in the trail. When he saw the outcropping shouldering out of the butte on his left, he halted the horse and dismounted, shoving his rifle in his saddle boot. Rummaging around in a saddlebag, he produced a leather thong, then tied the thong around the bay's front legs, hobbling the animal.

"Won't be long, Sweets," he told the horse, shucking his Henry from the boot.

He turned, walked to the base of the outcropping, and climbed through spindly stands of hawthorn and chokecherry. At the top he hunkered down behind rocks, removed his hat, and peered down the other side.

A stout log cabin hunkered in the trees along the base of the ridge, about fifty yards away. The cabin was weathered-gray, its roof disintegrating with age, so that the tin chimney lay nearly prone, belching thick smoke that drifted under the eaves, then rose and tore on the breeze.

East of the cabin was a corral made from new peeled logs. About twelve horses milled inside. On the top corral slat a trio of saddles, blankets, and bridles were draped. Stillman bet they hadn't been there long, and he bet those horses were still lathered from the long ride from the Majerus Rafter H ranch.

He gave a long study of the tiny shack, then of the terrain between him and the front door. Not much cover. But the way the cabin was situated, he could see only one window, in the wall facing obliquely from him.

With luck, he should be able to make it to the front door without being seen.

He gave Leon several minutes to get into position before lifting his rifle and waving it. Then he jacked a shell in the Henry's chamber, let the hammer down to half-cock, stood, and started down the slope, crouching and keeping the rifle out before him, avoiding large rocks and sage clumps.

He made it to the door and crouched beside it, waiting for his deputy. He didn't have to wait long. McMannigle came around the corner of the cabin, flushed from the run, holding his Spencer with the barrel pointed up. Stillman looked at him and mouthed, "One, two, three."

He kicked the door open and stepped to the side. "Freeze! You're under arrest!"

There were several curses and cries of anger. Boots thudded and chairs scraped the floor.

"Just stay where you are!" Leon shouted, covering the right side of the room while Stillman covered the left.

It took Stillman's eyes several seconds to adjust to the gloom within the cabin. He saw three vague human figures, one on a cot against the left wall, two near the wood stove. One of the men near the wood stove jerked his hand suddenly. Leon's rifle exploded, spitting flames and smoke, and the man crouched and fell back against the stove yelling, "Gaaaah!"

"No!" the other man by the stove yelled, throwing his arms over his face.

Stillman trained his rifle on the man on the cot. "We told you to freeze, you stupid bastards."

"I'm froze! I'm froze!" the man on the cot cried.

The man by the stove looked at his friend, who had slid down the right side of the stove to the floor, gurgling and grunting as though trying to say something. The sickening smell of burned flesh filled the cabin. "Good

Lord. . . ." the man by the stove said. His mouth dropped open as he stretched his thin, unshaven neck out, inspecting the wounded man. "That nigger shot Billy."

Leon said matter-of-factly, "He's gonna shoot you, too, if you don't shut your trap and drop your gunbelt."

"What for? We ain't done nothin'!"

"You ain't done nothin', eh, Miller?" Stillman said, recognizing the hardcase. "Let's see your bill of sale for those horses in the corral out yonder."

The tall, gangly Miller didn't say anything. His eyes rolled around stupidly.

"We didn't get none," the man on the cot said. His name was Lewis Free. He'd hauled freight for Hall's Mercantile a few months ago, then disappeared. "We bought 'em from some Injuns up in Canada."

"Lew, you're sayin' those horses aren't wearing the Rafter H brand?" Leon asked skeptically.

The two horse thieves looked at each other, faces turning petulant and grim as they realized their little horse-stealing enterprise had bitten the dust before it had even gotten started.

Stillman looked at Free, incredulity creasing the lawman's blue eyes set back in a brown, weathered face. "Who in the hell were you going to sell them to—that's what I'd like to know."

Free said nothing. Neither did Miller. The man on the floor gave a grunt, and sighed. Leon started moving toward him, his rifle aimed at Miller. Inadvertently, Leon kicked a can. The raucous clatter brought Stillman's head around. At the same time, out of the corner of the sheriff's eye, he saw Free move his right hand. Stillman lunged for the man and got there as Free brought his Colt to bear, cocking the hammer. Stillman grabbed the gun, which was aimed at his belly, just as Free tripped the trigger.

Stillman and Free both froze. As if in agonizing slowness, they watched the hammer start toward the firing pin. Stillman's stomach muscles clenched as he awaited the imminent bark and bullet. His eyes slitted as he winced, and his knees went numb. . . .

But nothing happened. The gun did not bark and no bullet ripped into Stillman's belly.

Then both men saw why. Stillman's hand had dropped over the gun at the same time the hammer had started forward. The webbed skin between the sheriff's thumb and index finger had intercepted the hammer about a quarter inch away from the firing pin.

Both men froze in their positions, staring at Stillman's hand pinned to the gun by the hammer. Then Free lifted his shocked eyes to Stillman's. His heart starting to beat again, Stillman grinned at the man, grabbed the gun away, and swung the butt of his rifle against Free's head, throwing him against the wall and laying him out cold.

The sheriff turned around and saw McMannigle and Miller regarding him warily. Stillman raised his left hand, the gun still clamped to the skin between his thumb and index finger.

Leon's eyes grew wide. He shook his head slowly and sighed. "That . . . that's cuttin' it close."

Stillman set his rifle butt down on the floor, leaned the barrel against his leg, and pulled back the revolver's hammer, releasing his hand from the gun. "Yeah . . . for a minute there I thought I heard angels."

Stillman and McMannigle got Miller and Free on two saddle horses, and tied the dead man to a third. Then they headed back toward Clantick, stopping at the Rafter H to inform the owner, Phil Majerus, that his horses were waiting for him in Moony's Coulee.

That done, they continued on the mail road for town,

Stillman taking the lead, the two prisoners and dead man following behind on lead ropes, McMannigle bringing up the rear. It was a quiet ride, the breeze picking up and the temperature dropping, the day turning gloomy as the clouds lowered. The weather reflected Stillman's mood as he thought about how close he'd come to taking a bullet.

He hadn't come that close since a drunk whore had back-shot him in a Virginia City brothel several years ago. The incident had forced him to retire his U.S. deputy marshal's badge. The surgeons had been unable to remove the bullet, which had snugged up dangerously close to his spine.

That had been a dark time in Stillman's life, and he'd started drinking heavily. Then he'd met his wife, Fay, who'd shown him the way back to daylight. His life had never been better than it was now, with his marriage to the only woman he'd ever truly loved. Before Fay, he'd been a loner, and lonely, though he hadn't realized it at the time. Fay had opened his mind and his heart, and his close call in the cabin had threatened to negate all of it. What was worse, it had nearly made his lovely Fay a widow.

He'd promised her before he'd taken the job as Hill County Sheriff that he'd never take any foolish risks, but the incident in the cabin had made him a liar. He'd gotten careless by not immediately disarming Free, and it had nearly cost him his life.

He shook his head and winced at the memory of the revolver's hammer starting its descent toward the firing pin, intercepted at the last possible moment by a quarter inch of flesh. Stillman was by nature a reflective man, but he'd been a top notch lawman for nearly twenty years because he'd put his duty ahead of his own personal safety. A few years ago he would have joked about such an incident as the one back in the cabin, and he would have slept well that night.

But now that he was married to Fay, his contemplative bent had become more pronounced. As he rode toward town with a stiff breeze at his back and a blood blister growing between his thumb and index finger, he was feeling downright skittish.

Maybe this was a job for another man, he reflected as the outlying shacks of Clantick rose from the dun prairie ahead of him. Maybe it was a job for a man who didn't have as much as Stillman had to lose. . . .

When he and McMannigle had their prisoners locked up in the jailhouse on First Street, the dead man taken over to Doc Evans, who doubled as an undertaker, and their horses secured in the stable behind the jail, McMannigle went to the window and peered out at the ever-darkening afternoon.

He said, "Look here."

Stillman was stoking the wood stove. He closed the door, set the poker in the kindling box, and walked to the window. A fine snow was falling over First Street, dusting the horses waiting in the wagon traces before Sam Wa's cafe.

"Here it comes," Stillman said darkly.

"I reckon Doc was right."

Stillman sighed and grabbed his hat off the peg by the door. He still wore his coat, since the jailhouse had not yet heated and wouldn't be adequately warm for another twenty minutes. "Will you keep the stove stoked for our prisoners back there?" he asked his deputy. "I'm going to see if Fay's home. She went out to the Hawley farm for a birthday party. I'm hoping she saw the storm coming and hightailed it home."

"I'll be here," Leon said. "I reckon my date's off. Can't go traipsing across the river in this weather."

"Sorry about that, ol' buddy," Stillman said. "Anyone I know?"

Leon beamed, hooking his thumbs behind his cartridge belt. "Miss Emily Norton."

"Emily Norton?" Stillman said, amazed. "The widow from up Pine Creek?"

"One and the same," McMannigle said, still grinning.

Stillman poked up the brim of his hat and scrutinized the deputy disbelievingly. "Why, she's about as pretty as they come around here—and *rich*!"

"You're right about that, Ben." Leon snickered.

Stillman probed McMannigle's eyes. "How in the hell do you do it, anyway? What do you have that others don't?" He was referring to all the women who'd fallen in love with the handsome black man, only to have their hearts broken because Leon wasn't yet ready to settle down. But why should he? After all, he roomed in a brothel for free.

Leon snickered again, dropping his chin and shaking his head. "I'll just leave that up to the ladies to decide . . . if you get my drift, Sheriff."

Stillman shook his head and laughed, turning for the door. "I reckon," he said.

"Say hi to Fay."

"I will . . . if she's home."

With that, Stillman closed the door behind him and turned left up the boardwalk, heading east toward French Street, where he and Fay lived in a little, two-story white frame house encircled by a picket fence and flanked by a buggy shed and chicken coop. Stillman had loved chickens since raising them back in Pennsylvania as a boy, and he'd started raising them again after he'd retired his deputy marshal's badge. When he and Fay had moved back to Clantick last spring, he'd started another flock after adding the chicken coop to the stable house.

He went around to the back door and entered the kitchen. All was mid-afternoon dark; no lamps had been lit, and the stove was cold.

"Fay?" he called, halfheartedly, sensing she wasn't home.

He checked all the rooms just to be sure, then went out the front door and stood on the porch, watching the snow fall. Beyond the white roofs of the town, the Two Bear Mountains stood cloaked in clouds.

Unease crept up Stillman's spine. He'd wanted so much to find her home, but she wasn't here. She was out there, in those cloud-buried mountains.

He had a mind to ride out after her but, hell, she'd probably be home any minute. Besides, she was a big girl and knew the Two Bears as well as he did.

He sighed and rubbed the festering hammer cut between his thumb and index finger, suppressing his anxiety. Then he went inside to build a fire in the kitchen range and start a pot of coffee.

5

THE FAST-FORMING STORM slid over the mountains and descended upon the Hawley cabin with a speed no less astonishing for being relatively common in the northern Rockies. Candace was the first to see the snow, but by the time she'd called it to the grown-ups' attention, a good inch had already covered the porch, and the southern peaks of the mountains were lost in gauzy white. Even the barn was a dim outline through the slanting flakes, which the wind was starting to swirl across the barnyard.

"Oh, my gosh," Fay said, bending to look out the low window, the others huddled around her. "I should have been keeping an eye on the weather."

"Well, jeepers," Jody said, "I looked out no more than fifteen, twenty minutes ago, just before Candace was getting ready to open her presents, and I swear the clouds were a mile high—and thin!"

Shaking his head, Earl Hawley said, "I reckon I lived in this country long enough to know when a storm's on the way."

"You can't live in this country that long, Earl," Crystal said. She was standing beside Fay, one arm on her friend's shoulders, the other hand on her own distended belly, and peering out at the bright whiteness that made her blue eyes sparkle.

"I bet we could make it home; I got stock to feed," Jody said.

"Don't you try it, young man," Mrs. Hawley warned him. She turned from the window to add a log to the kitchen stove. "You know what happened to Adam Broughton two winters ago. Tried racing one of these late-winter storms back from Big Sandy, and they didn't find him until July—six miles off the main road!"

"Doreen's right, Jody," Fay said. "It's thickening up fast out there. I'd like to head back to town—I know Ben's going to be worried—but I know there's a good chance I won't make it." She turned to Mrs. Hawley, who was filling a percolator with water from a five-gallon bucket on the cupboard. "I think we all better stay right here until this thing blows itself out."

"That's right," Doreen nodded. "You all just stay right where you are. I'll put some more coffee on. Earl, you better make sure we have plenty of wood up on the porch. Never know how long one of these clippers will last."

"I'll get right on it, dear," Earl said, reaching for his coat. "I better bring up another quarter of that beef I butchered day before last, too."

"I'll help you, Earl," Jody said.

"Yippee!" Candace cried, clapping her hands and lifting up and down on the toes of her black patten shoes. She grinned merrily at Fay. "We'll all stay right here and tell stories all night long!"

Fay smiled tensely, and looked out the window, where Earl and Jody were heading across the yard toward the barn, the black and white collie dog following a few steps behind, its shaggy, burr-laden coat covered with snow.

"I wish I could be as happy about this as you are, child," Fay said, thinking how worried Ben would be, disgusted with herself for not keeping a closer eye on the weather.

It was a half hour later, and they were all sitting at the Hawley's kitchen table playing a quiet game of cards, grown-ups and child alike, when above the moaning wind they heard the dog bark and a horse whinny.

In the red frame house that served as both living quarters and office for Clyde Evans, M.D., the doctor awoke with a start. Blinking his eyes, he found himself lying on the parlor settee, a volume of Keats open on his lap, an empty goblet lying on his belly, a wet stain on his shirt.

"Shit," he groused, inspecting the stain, which smelled of cheap brandy.

He remembered sitting down to read and drink. He'd read a few of his favorite sonnets, finished the glass, poured another, and started "Ode to a Grecian Urn." He must have fallen asleep halfway through the poem, a testament to his languor. He'd been sleepy all day, having been awakened at two a.m. to set a drunken cowboy's broken nose.

The rapping, which had awakened him, sounded again, rattling the sashed windows in the door. Grumbling, Evans pushed himself to a sitting position, letting the book and glass fall to the floor with a thunk and a clatter.

"Coming, goddamnit . . . I'm coming." He stood and blinked the sleep from his eyes. Evans was a medium-sized man with the rounded shoulders of a boxer, thick red hair, and a heavy walrus mustache, the wry man's only nod to ostentation. His shabby dress shirt, worn whipcord trousers, and stained wool vest made him look more like a down-and-out gambler than a doctor, and his abrasive demeanor did nothing to temper the resemblance.

He halfheartedly shoved his wrinkled shirttails into his pants, and shuffled to the door, his untied shoelaces whipping about his feet and clattering on the floor. His caller knocked again, louder.

"I'm coming, for God sakes . . . keep your pants on," the doctor grumbled as he opened the door.

When he saw the tall, severe-looking woman standing before him in a long wool coat and fashionable otterskin hat, Evans did not bother to hide his regret.

"Oh, no . . . it's you."

"Hello, Doctor," Katherine Kemmet said coolly.

"To what or whom do I owe the honor?"

"Mrs. Nelson. Her water broke. She sent her eldest son for us."

Evans winced like a boy who'd just been asked to empty slop buckets. "It's snowing, for God sakes," he complained, looking at the flakes falling on the lady's leather-upholstered, red-wheeled buggy parked outside his sagging picket fence. He glanced up at the sky, the color of a lamp over which a soiled sheet had been thrown. "Hell, it's going to storm."

Katherine Kemmet kept both hands in the rabbit muffler held at her waist, and regarded the doctor like an Army sergeant. "Yes, we'd better hurry. You'd better bring an overnight bag. We could very well be stranded at the Nelson ranch."

Evans stood glaring at the thin, gray-eyed, pale-skinned woman, flabbergasted by her bravery and a little unnerved by her devotion to her job. He tried to come up with some excuse for staying home, but to no avail. Mrs. Nelson had been having a troubled pregnancy. It was his duty as the woman's doctor to do everything he could to deliver her child. With Katherine's help, of course.

Since she and her husband, a Lutheran pastor who had died last spring from a stroke, had come to Clantick three years ago, she'd helped Evans with most of the problematic deliveries around the county. Katherine was a midwife by profession, and a damn good one, but Evans didn't care for the woman personally. She was everything you'd expect in a Lutheran pastor's wife— pious, persnickety, judgmental, and querulous. A drinker and a notorious lech, Evans got along with Katherine Kemmet about as well as kerosene got along with fire.

"Ah . . . shit," Evans said, never one to censor himself in front of ladies, "come in, come in."

He threw the door wide for Katherine, then turned and stomped around several rooms, grumbling and cursing under his breath as he gathered his doctor's bag, a buffalo coat, a pair of heavy mittens, and a ragged rabbit hat with earflaps. Meanwhile, Katherine stood in the foyer, reprimanding him for the poor condition of his house.

"You're a professional, Doctor. Why not live like one?"

He returned to the foyer looking like an Alaskan prospector in a Yukon tavern. "Because I'm just a poor country sawbones," he said absently, looking around for the small pistol he carried on out-of-town trips, "and my patients wouldn't care if I practiced in a barn."

"The Lord smiles upon neatness."

"Then tell him to send a maid."

"I swear, Doctor—you're absolutely imbecilic at times!"

"Fire me . . . please."

"Oh!" she exclaimed, rolling her eyes at his customary

nonsense. She regarded the book and glass lying on the floor by the settee. "I see you haven't been making good on your promise to stop drinking. . . ."

Evans found his pistol under a stack of illustrated magazines and an ashtray spilling cigar butts. "It's my only comfort in life," he said, checking the gun for ammunition. "That and Mrs. Lee's whores."

Katherine Kemmet pursed her lips. "I'm not going to let you rile me, Clyde. That's what you want, though, isn't it?"

"Yes, Katherine, it is."

"Why?"

"Cheap entertainment." Evans smiled ironically and stuffed the gun in his coat pocket. He glanced out the window again and shook his head darkly.

He gestured at the door. "Shall we?"

Stillman sat at his oilcloth-covered table, big hands wrapped around a smoking mug, brows ridged in troubled thought.

Half an hour had passed since he'd come home to an empty house. To his left, a sashed window framed with gingham curtains shone gray. It was getting darker by the minute, and the snow was getting thicker, building on the window ledge and on the chicken coop and buggy house beyond.

Stillman peered at the window, then at the wall clock.

Damn . . . where was she?

He winced and shook his head. He slid his chair out, stood, and reached for his hat and buckskin coat. He shrugged into his coat, donned his hat, and stuffed a wool scarf into one of the buckskin's deep pockets. Turning for the door, he remembered something. He picked up a leather mitt from the table and used it to move the coffeepot from the range to the warming rack.

Then he blew out the lantern on the wall over the table, opened the door, and headed outside.

By the time he approached the jailhouse on First Street he was covered with snow and chilled to the bone. Opening the door, he stepped into the jailhouse with his shoulders hunched and his face screwed up against the cold. He removed his hat and shook the snow from its brim. Leon was sitting at the desk near the ticking stove, cleaning his revolver.

"What brings you back?" he asked, looking up from his work as Stillman headed for the rifle rack on the opposite wall.

"Fay's not home."

Leon thought about this, his black eyes growing blacker. "Damn! You think she's stuck at the Hawleys'?"

"I don't know, but I aim to find out," Stillman said, unlocking the padlocked chain over the gun rack.

"You ain't goin' *out* there?" Leon said, as though he couldn't believe what he'd heard.

"That's exactly what I'm doing." The sheriff removed his Henry rifle from the rack and stood it against the wall.

"That's crazy, Ben. Look at it snow out there. Hell, you can't see more than thirty feet. And it's gettin' cold!"

"She isn't home, Leon. What else can I do?"

Leon stood and walked over to Stillman, who was snapping the padlock closed. "Chances are she saw the storm comin', and knowin' how fast it can get bad in the mountains, she decided to stay at the Hawley place till it blows itself out."

Stillman chewed his mustache, thinking.

"Jeff Chandler just hauled a freight load in from Big Sandy," Leon continued, "and he said this clipper's the worst he's seen—and Jeff's been haulin' freight around here for fifteen years. You can't go out in that. You wouldn't make it more than a mile!"

Stillman turned and walked to the window, rubbing his jaw. Leon was right. It was getting bad out there. He could just barely make out Sam Wa's cafe across the street. Like Leon had said, Fay had most likely seen the storm coming and, knowing she couldn't outrun it, had remained with the Hawleys.

Leon moved up beside him and put a hand on his shoulder. "What do you say we play a little poker? I just got paid, and those girls over at Mrs. Lee's haven't had a chance to tap me yet."

Stillman stared glumly out the window. He knew he wouldn't be able to strike all doubts that Fay was safe, but he also knew there was nothing he could do about it just now. He'd have to wait out the storm for her. His heart ached, his stomach felt queasy, and he knew it was going to be one hell of a long night.

He turned to Leon with a troubled sigh and said, "Deal 'em."

6

IN THE HAWLEY kitchen, Jody Harmon set his cards down on the table, beside his coffee cup, and looked at Earl. Earl was frowning and listening, as was everyone else at the table. It was definitely a horse's whinny they had heard.

Doreen Hawley glanced at her husband. "Earl, are all the horses in the barn?"

"Should be," Earl said, setting his cards down flat and sliding back his chair. " 'Less one got out . . . but I shut those doors up tight."

He got up and walked to a window just as a muffled voice called above the wind, "Hello, the house."

Everyone in the kitchen gave a start. Earl peered through the window, frowning. He turned to Jody. "Four men on horses. Musta got caught in the storm."

Jody glanced at Crystal and Fay, and Doreen Hawley. "You ladies stay put. Earl and I'll check it out." He stood, retrieved his gunbelt off a peg by the door, and wrapped it around his waist.

Earl grabbed his Winchester from behind the table, and jacked a shell in the breech. "Prob'ly just some cowboys got caught out too far from their headquarters, but you never know out here," he said to Jody.

"You two be careful," Crystal warned.

Earl opened the door and both men stepped outside. Jody closed the door behind them, hunching his shoulders against the blast of cold wind and snow and casting his gaze off the porch. Before him four snow-covered men sat four snow-covered horses, men and horses looking frozen to the bone. All Jody could make out of the men's faces beneath their snow-laden hats were white eyebrows and mustaches.

"Mind if we hole up here till the storm blows out?" one of them inquired above the wind. "We're about froze solid!"

Earl cast Jody an uneasy look, and headed off the porch. "Follow me," he yelled to the riders, walking toward the barn, keeping his head low to avoid the full thrust of the storm.

The visitors dismounted their horses stiffly, and followed Earl, leading their mounts by the reins. Jody brought up the rear, squinting his eyes against the stinging, wind-whipped snow.

In the barn, Earl lit a lantern and hung it on a beam, and he and Jody helped the men unsaddle their horses. The saddle buckles were so cold, they hurt to touch. The newcomers themselves were so cold that about all they could do was stamp their feet and beat their hands against their backs, their frosty breath rising to the rafters.

When Jody and Earl had the tack put up and the horses penned with hay, oats, and water, Earl turned to the men shivering in the shadows. "Well, I don't have no heat out here—you'll have to join us in the house."

"Much obliged," one of them said, teeth chattering, head hunkered down in his coat. His saddlebags were draped over his shoulder. "I'll bring these in with me, if you don't mind. Don't want the mice gettin' at the pretties I bought for my girl."

Earl led the way to the house, and Jody brought up the rear, unwilling to give these men his back. He knew most of the cowboys who worked on the surrounding ranches, and none of these men looked familiar.

Earl mounted the porch, where a drift was building, and opened the door. He stepped aside as the newcomers entered. As Jody stepped past Earl, they locked looks, their eyes warning each other to keep their guards up. Earl followed Jody inside, closing the door behind them, but not before a gust of snow blew in and powdered the puncheon floor.

The newcomers immediately struggled out of their frozen overcoats and headed for the two wood stoves, which Earl stoked until they fairly roared, the wind blowing over the chimneys making an especially good draw. Crystal and Fay sat at the table, one on either side of Candace, regarding the visitors warily. Doreen Hawley was working at the stove, rewarming a roast and slicing potatoes into a skillet.

Whooping and sighing, the men basked in the heat from the stoves, turning this way and that and rubbing their shoulders and arms, beating blood back into their limbs.

"Oooh, doggie, does that feel good!" one of them exclaimed, a muscular wire of a man with a sharp-featured face and a silver front tooth. "I thought we were going to die out there for sure!" He looked around the room with frank curiosity, his glazed eyes finding Crystal and Fay and lingering there a little longer than Jody was comfortable with.

He walked over and stood protectively behind the two women, one hand on the chair back of each. "Been out there a while, I take it," he said to the wiry man conversationally.

"The storm just kinda snuck up us on us. One minute the sky was clear, the next minute we was gettin' pelted with sleet."

Jody glanced at the two men standing before the other stove—a big, shaggy-headed, baby-faced beast and a tall, thin man with a deeply pitted face. The latter eyed the women as he warmed his hands behind his back, and said nothing. Exuberantly, the big man said, "Just like Wayne said—one minute the sky was clear, and the next minute we was gettin' sleeted on. Why, I thought—!"

"That's enough, Benji," the wiry man said. "I think they get the point." To Jody, he said, "Benji here's not shootin' with a full load, if you get what I mean. Sometimes I have to be a little rude to shut him up."

He glanced coldly at Benji, who just frowned at him, vaguely hurt.

"My name's Wayne. That there next to Benji is T. J." He jerked his thumb at the older, thickset man standing beside him. "This here's Tony. We sure appreciate you folks takin' us in like this. You don't know how good I felt when I saw the light in your window."

"It's not a good night to be out," Jody said, hoping for an explanation as to what the men had been up to.

Cowmen were always drifting in and out of the country, but rarely in the winter, when they were either employed or holed up in bawdy houses until spring. Jody didn't like the looks of this crew, and not just because they didn't look familiar, either. They could have been out-of-work cowboys, but none of them really had the rope-scarred hands or deeply weathered faces of that breed. There was a brashness about them, as well, a subtle arrogance uncommon in your typical range-popper, most of whom were extremely humble and in-gratiating.

"No, it ain't," Wayne said. He offered no explanation, just a faint smile of complicity that told Jody the man knew what he was fishing for.

The man named T. J. said, "Well, Wayne told you our handles. Who might you folks be . . . and the two la-dies?" With this last, his eyes lighted on Fay and Crystal and seemed to pause there.

Jody swung around to look at the man. He was as wiry and muscular as Wayne, but taller. Although his wool shirt and denim breeches were little more than rags, the gun and holster he wore tied down on his hip appeared in extremely good condition, telling Jody that the man placed a high value on his weapons and that he was probably handy with the well-oiled forty-five. The man's savage face and eyes and his apparent gun prow-ess made Jody nervous, especially since Jody's pregnant wife was stranded in the same cabin with the man, and also since Jody considered himself about as good with a pistol as your average saddlebum: He could hit your occasional rattlesnake but little else.

Jody said, "That there's Earl Hawley. He owns this place. The woman tending the stove is his wife, Doreen. Candace here's their daughter. This is my wife, Crystal, and this is Fay—" Jody looked at Fay and stopped, not sure he should tell these men her last name. Since they looked like outlaws, they might have tangled with Ben. If they held a grudge, they could possibly take it out on Fay.

Fay's eyes flickered questioningly at Jody. Instantly she seemed to intuit his quandary, and turned to the new-comers. "Fay Beaumont," she said, using her maiden name. "Pleased to make your acquaintance."

Candace swung her head to Fay, a puzzled expression

on her face. Before Candace could say anything, Jody thought he detected Crystal's hand going to the girl's thigh beneath the table, effectively hushing the child.

"Beaumont, eh?" Wayne said. "That's a right pretty name . . . for a right pretty woman."

"Thank you."

"Beaumont, uh?" the older man said speculatively. "Don't I know that name? Sure, there was a Beaumont ranchin' down around Milestown a few years back."

"That would be my father, Alex," Fay said. "Our home place was down along the Yellowstone."

"Sure enough—I remember now," Tony said. "I was workin' for a spread in the area at the time. You musta been in your teens. Boy, you sure turned some heads and got the boys talkin'!" He laughed, then caught himself. "Uh . . . excuse me, ma'am. I didn't mean to offend or nothin'."

"No offense taken."

"What are you doin' up in these parts, if you don't mind me askin'?"

"I teach school. Candace is my student. It's her birthday."

Wayne stared at her dully. Then he grinned. "That's nice. A birthday party. I like that."

"So do I," Fay said, flashing a smile at Candace.

Jody had to admire her spleen, but at the same time her friendliness made him uneasy, and he was glad when Doreen turned from the range. "I'll fill some plates for you men, if you want to have a seat at the table."

"Much obliged, ma'am," Tony said, rubbing his thick hands together hungrily.

While the newcomers ate at the table, the others sat in the living room—Fay, Crystal, and Candace on the settee, and Earl and Jody in two homemade, hide-covered rockers. Doreen manned the table, refilling plates and coffee cups. No one said anything, the new-comers too involved with their grub for idle conversation.

Jody watched them uneasily, glancing outside now and then. The sun was going down and the wind howled like banshees. Snow raked the windows.

The older man appeared the least harmless of the four-some. The big man's sheer size made him dangerous, but probably not as dangerous as Wayne and the pock-faced man with the coyote eyes named T. J. If there was going to be trouble, it would undoubtedly be initiated by them. Those were the two to watch.

Jody sighed and listened to the wind in the stovepipe, watching Doreen Hawley dish up thick slices of Candace's birthday cake and set them before the unshaven men at the table. Crystal and Fay spoke in hushed tones while Candace read a book, silently moving her lips.

Earl dozed, then came awake suddenly with a snort. "Game o' cribbage?" he asked Jody.

Jody shrugged. "Why not?"

Earl got up to retrieve his cribbage board and cards. As he did so, his rocker rocked back against the wall, dislodging something from a peg, which reported a heavy thump as it hit the floor. Jody turned and saw Wayne's saddlebags on the floor beside Earl's chair. Spilling from one of the open flaps were three bundles of greenbacks.

"Well, I'll be . . ." Earl said.

Instinctively sensing the sudden danger, Jody reached for the gun on his hip, but before he could clear the holster he heard, "You do that, slick . . . you just bring that pistol right on out of there."

Looking toward the kitchen, he saw the business end of Wayne's revolver aimed at his head.

7

THERE WERE TWO seconds of dead silence, Jody sitting in his rocker frozen, his hand on the butt of his revolver. Earl stood about ten feet in front of him, lifting his gaze from the saddlebags to Wayne's gun, the big farmer's mouth hanging open in shock.

Jody didn't turn his head to look at Crystal, Fay, and Candace, sitting on the settee to his right. But he knew from their sudden silence that they were as paralyzed as he was.

All the men at the table had turned their heads to Jody with expressions varying from disdain to mockery. Doreen Hawley turned from the cupboard behind them. Seeing the gun, she gasped and shattered a cup on the floor.

"Go on, hayseed," Wayne said to Jody. "Bring that pistol out of that holster . . . nice and slow. Set it here on the table."

Jody stood, eased the pistol out of his holster, only touching the grips, and set it on the table. "Look," he said, "I don't know what you men are up to, and I don't want to know. We have women and a child here, and we don't want any trouble."

"You don't want any trouble, huh?" Wayne said, tonguing a tooth musingly. 'Well, you wouldna' had any trouble if the big clod there hadn't messed with my saddlebags."

Earl was red-faced with anger, his big hands balled at his sides. "This is my house . . . you put that gun away."

"Sit down, Earl, or I'll put a hole in ya," Wayne said casually.

Earl stiffly stood his ground, bent slightly forward at the waist. "This is my house. I won't have guns drawn in my house."

"Earl!" Doreen cried. She stood behind the table, her back to the cupboards, her face ashen, eyes wide with fear.

Behind him, Jody heard Candace give a muted cry. Fay whispered consolingly, hushing the girl.

Wayne turned to the big, baby-faced man on his right. "Benji, tie Earl to his rockin' chair."

"Okay, Wayne," Benji said, scraping his chair back. "You better sit down in that chair like Wayne says," he said to Earl, pointing at the rocker.

Earl stared furiously at Wayne, whose right elbow was propped on the oilcloth, beside a half-eaten piece of birthday cake, the gun in his hand pointed at Earl's belly. The man called T. J. and the older man, Tony, were grinning like they were watching a melodrama staged for their own personal amusement.

"Earl!" Doreen cried again, louder. Her voice cracked and her eyes shone with terror.

"Daddy," Candace sobbed.

Jody said, "Do like he says, Earl. It'll be all right."

"I don't cotton to this . . . not at all," Earl snarled. "You come into my house, eat my food—"

"Sit down or die, Earl . . . the choice is yours!" Wayne shouted, nearly coming out of his chair.

"Earl, sit down, for God sakes!" Crystal exclaimed.

Earl's large, raw-boned body slowly, grudgingly relaxed. His hands unclenched. The farmer sighed heavily, turned, walked over to the rocking chair, and turned back around. He stared at Wayne coldly for several more seconds, and sank into the chair with a grunt and a curse.

"Tie him," Wayne snapped at Benji, who was a full head taller than Earl.

Benji looked vaguely around. "With what?"

Wayne reached behind him, grabbed Doreen's arm, and pulled her out in front of him. She gave a scream and cried.

"Mama!" Candace screamed, starting from the settee. Fay held her back, pressing Candace's head against her breast.

"Get him some rope," Wayne told the woman.

"I-I don't have any. . . ." the woman sobbed, looking around as tears rolled down her cheeks, absently smoothing her apron with her hands.

"Don't tell me you don't have any rope," Wayne said. "This is a farm, ain't it?"

"Only rope's in the barn," Earl growled defiantly.

"Look around for some rope," Wayne told Benji. "If you don't find none, grab a sheet off a bed and tear it into strips. I want him tied." He glanced at Jody. "I want them both tied."

Benji opened the door to the back of the house, which was an add-on to the original squatter's shack, and stepped through. "Close the door—we don't need to heat the whole damn shack!" Wayne scolded him. Benji came back, his clodhopper boots booming on the board floor, and closed the door behind him.

Jody stood before the table, hearing the storm outside and Benji's big boots clomping around in the back of the house. Candace sobbed against Fay's breast. Fay cooed to the child soothingly, rocking her gently.

Jody glanced at the three men around the table, all of them watching him with mild amusement, enjoying the fear they saw in his face. He was aware of his gun on the table, only about four feet in front of him, and he considered reaching for it, but not for long. He'd never been handy with a handgun, and he chastised himself now for not working with the weapon out behind his cabin, plugging tin cans, honing his aim and dexterity. This was a rough land and a man had to be good with a handgun if he wanted to protect his family. He should have learned that after his father was killed. But he hadn't, and here he stood, only a few measly feet away from his gun and unable to do anything with it but get himself killed.

In a few minutes he'd be tied and even more helpless than he was right now . . . even more incapable of protecting his pregnant wife and these other women and young Candace.

He glanced at Crystal, sitting on the settee, her face blanched with fear. She must have read the frustration in his eyes, because she tried an encouraging smile. The thunder of Benji's boots grew louder, the door opened, and the big man appeared, grinning and holding up several strips torn from a white cotton bedsheet.

"I tore up a sheet, just like you said, Wayne."

"Very good. Now tie up these two sons of bitches." Wayne cut his eyes to the women. "Sorry for the French, but what do you expect . . . opening your doors to four strangers in a storm?" He grinned.

"You're pathetic," Crystal told him.

Wayne only smiled, and sat back in his chair, staring at Crystal bemusedly. "You're right pretty."

"Don't say anything, Crystal," Jody said. "Just don't say a thing." Crystal had a mouth on her, and it had been known to cause her grief. Right now she needed to be as quiet and meek as she could be. Standing out amidst these three men would only get her into trouble, and there'd be nothing Jody could do to save her.

"Right purty," Wayne said.

"Both those women are pretty," T. J. Cross said. "And the girl, too."

As Benji tied his wrists together with the cloth, Jody glared at the men at the table. The ragged, hard-faced firebrands sat amidst the dirty plates and cups as if they owned the place, staring lasciviously at Crystal and Fay . . . as if they owned them, too.

At length, Wayne tore his gaze from the women. "Tie him tight, Benjie," he said. His eyes smoldered darkly as his eyes resettled on the women. "Good and tight."

Twenty miles northeast of the Hawley farm, the Nelson ranch sat in a broad horseshoe of the Milk River. Nils Nelson had done well since coming into the country twelve years ago. His cabin was not the usual ramshackle found hereabouts, but a solid, two-story barrack with a wide front porch and a big, fieldstone hearth. There were several outbuildings, including a handsome frame barn and a bunkhouse flanking the cabin, and several acres of interconnecting corrals presided over by a windmill.

Under most circumstances, the headquarters owned an undisputable air of permanence and relative wealth. Tonight, however, racked by the wind and bludgeoned by the snow, it more resembled a rowboat in an ocean squall. Here, where few trees and hills broke the wind or stopped the snow, the buildings were all but buried. If you looked from the bunkhouse to the house or vice versa, you'd be hard pressed to see a light behind the heavy, steadily growing drifts that the wind sculpted into frozen waves, complete with frothy curlicues at the tops.

No one was looking out the windows of either structure at the moment, however. The three hired men were playing cards in the bunkhouse, as close to the roaring stove as they could get without getting burned. Dr. Evans and the midwife, Katherine Kemmet, were in the house delivering a baby while the baby's mother screamed and thrashed miserably, and the baby's half brother paced in the hall. Nils Nelson himself was stranded in Chinook, where he and his foreman had gone earlier in the day for supplies.

When the baby finally came, it was a great relief to the mother as well as the doctor and midwife. The umbilical cord had been wrapped around the baby's neck, and had come very close to hanging the child as the mother's expanding and contracting uterus had forced it down the birth canal. Dr. Evans had diagnosed the problem and had wasted no time in shoving a hand into the canal and working the cord over the baby's head with his fingers.

Katherine Kemmet gave a great sigh of relief as the doctor handed her the wailing, viscera-covered infant for cleaning. "Good work, Doctor."

"All in a day's toil."

"This child would have died if you hadn't been here."

"One less bird in the flock, one less ragamuffin at the feeding trough," Evans grumbled, wiping his bloody hands on a towel.

Katherine's face registered shock and anger, even more than usual. She started to speak, but the mother, Nils Nelson's young second wife—his first had died two years ago from a cancer—cleared her throat to speak. "What . . . what is it, Katherine?"

Toweling the crying infant in her arms, Katherine turned to the wan, sweat-soaked mother in the big, four-poster bed. "Why, it's a girl, Alice—just what you wanted!"

"Is—is it all right?"

"It's beautiful!" Katherine cried, shooting the doctor a meaningful glance. "Just beautiful . . . and what a miracle!"

As Katherine handed the child to Alice Nelson, Evans said, "It'll be a miracle if I ever get a drink tonight." He wrapped his bloody tools in a towel and headed for the door.

"Where are you going, Doctor?" Katherine asked.

"My job is done. Call me if you must, but only if you must." He opened the door and walked into the hall. Turning, he nearly ran into Ned Nelson, Nils's youngest boy by his first marriage.

"How's the baby, Doc?" the big, rawboned lad asked eagerly. Seventeen, he was the only son Nelson had been able to keep home to groom for taking over the ranch.

"Just fine, Ned, just fine. You have a sister."

"A sister?" the boy exclaimed. "A sister's just what Pa's been wantin'—after four boys!"

"Well, he's got one now," Evans said distractedly.

"When can I see her?"

"Tomorrow, my boy—the baby and mother are a mite tired out." Evans wrapped an arm around the young man's shoulders and started toward the stairs. "Say, Ned—I have a little problem, and I was wondering if you might help me out."

"What's that, Dr. Evans?" Ned asked as he and Evans descended the stairs.

"I seem to have forgotten the whiskey flask I usually keep in my medical kit—and I was wondering if your father might have a stash in the house somewhere. I like to have a swig when I'm finished with a patient . . . just to calm my nerves, if you know what I'm saying."

"Well, sure, Doc . . . Pa has a liquor cabinet in his study."

"A whole cabinet?" Evans said with eager anticipation. Then, trying to recover some dignity, he added, "I mean, of course . . . a cabinet. Well, if you'd just point me in the right direction . . . ?"

"Right through that door, Doc. I guess I'll be headin' back out to the bunkhouse for the night."

Evans had turned toward the kitchen, where he intended to deposit the bloody tools wrapped in his towel. He stopped and regarded Ned dubiously. "What's that you say, Ned? The bunkhouse?"

Ned nodded. "That's where I've been bunkin' since I turned sixteen. Pa says it's best for me to sleep with the foreman and the other men . . . you know, to pick up little tricks of the trade here and there and, as Pa says, 'to rub some o' the velvet off my horns.' "

"Why, it's storming out there, Ned!"

"Oh, I tied a rope from the house to the bunkhouse when I seen it was gettin' thick. Pa always has me do that anyways, before a storm . . . in case we need the men for anything. I'll be all right, Doc. I'll just follow the rope." Ned was shrugging into a heavy wool coat, from the pocket of which protruded a gray stocking cap. "I've got all the wood boxes loaded and all the stoves stoked. You and Miss Kemmet can bunk wherever you want—there's plenty o' empty rooms in the house since my brothers left. You can even cozy up in the study, Doc. Pa has a mess o' books in there with his liquor, and I know how you're a book-readin' man." The boy pulled the stocking cap over his head. "You'll just want to keep the stoves stoked—that's all."

"Well . . . all right, Ned," Evans said with a feigned sigh of apprehension. He couldn't believe he was actually going to have Nils Nelson's liquor cabinet and study full of books all to himself! Katherine could be a problem, but she'd be busy most of the night with Mrs. Nelson and the baby. "You be careful out there, and good night to you, son."

"Good night, Doc," Ned said as he drew on his second mitten and opened the outside door, through which an icy blast of wind and snow blew. Ned stepped out, wrestled the door closed behind him, and was gone, leaving a good shovelful of snow melting on the foyer rug at Clyde Evans's feet.

"Well, I'll be goddamned," the doctor said, feeling like a kid in a candy shop. Katherine Kemmet might have gotten him stranded in a storm seven miles from town . . . seven chilblain miles from his books and his booze. But he'd make do, by God.

He'd make do.

8

IN THE HAWLEY kitchen, under a cloud of cigarette and cigar smoke, Wayne Adler stared at the cards in his hand. The game was draw poker, jacks or better to open, check and raise permitted. The ante was ten dollars, with no betting limits, and all the raises your little heart desired.

It was a rich man's game, and why not? Were not Adler and his *compañeros* rich men? The stolen greenbacks, which the men had divvied up between them, lay in neat stacks before them, as irrefutable evidence of their wealth. All they needed now were beautiful women in low-cut gowns, fancy store-bought duds, Tennessee whiskey, and Cuban cigars—all of which they would indeed have as soon as the storm let up and they made it to Canada. Calgary was hopping these days, Adler had heard, and he intended to hop right along with it. He'd stomp through the winter with his tail up, then head for Mexico come spring.

For now, though, he was stuck here in this granger's motley kitchen, smoking his cheap tobacco and playing with Tony Riemersma's tattered, whiskey-stained cards, the backs of which bore pictures of bare-breasted women. The women were a chronic distraction to Benji, and Adler and the other players used it to their best advantage. They knew that if the shaggy-headed idiot stared long enough at the backs of the cards rather than at the faces, it was entirely possible to win most if not all of his plunder.

"Come on, Wayne," T. J. Cross said. "Shit or get off the pot."

"Keep your goddamn pants on," Wayne said, throwing a card and picking up another.

"You men have to use that kind of language?" Earl asked them. He was still tied to his rocking chair, a few feet from Jody, and he was still mad. "There's women and a child present."

Candace was now sitting on her mother's lap, in a Windsor chair beside the sitting room's stove, a buffalo blanket draped over her legs. Fay and Crystal were on the settee. Crystal had grown fatigued, so Fay had insisted she lie down and rest her feet on Fay's lap. The sitting room was dark except for the glow around the stove's doors, while the kitchen was lit by three lanterns—one on the cupboard and two hanging from a ceiling beam. It gave the outlaws, sitting around the table playing cards, an eerie, theatrical quality. Their shadows stretched wide across the table and floor.

"Yeah, we have to use language like that, Earl," Wayne said, eyeing his cards. "We're outlaws. That's how outlaws talk." He leaned toward Benji, showing the man the back of one of his pasteboards. "Lookee here, Benji . . . look at the teats on this one."

"Those aren't nothin' compared to the ones o' that blonde I just threw down."

"How do you think they'd compare to the teats on the

teacher sittin' in the other room?" T. J. Cross asked Benji.

The big man looked into the semi-dark sitting room. He hesitated. "Well . . . I don't know. She has her clothes on."

The others laughed so hard they almost fell out of their chairs.

When he'd finally regained his breath, Wayne said, "Maybe we should ask her if she'd show us. What do you think about that, Benji?"

Benji looked embarrassed. He stared hard at his cards, hunching his shoulders. "I—I don't think she'd do that, Wayne."

"Well, what if I made her?"

"I-I don't think that'd be right . . . makin' a lady take her clothes off if she don't want to."

Tony slapped the table and howled with Adler and Cross.

When Adler had caught his breath, he turned to Benji. "You beat men so bad you couldn't make heads or tails of their faces—crushed a fella's skull with your *hands!*—but you don't think it'd be right to make a woman take her clothes off?"

Benji's eyes slid around the table. "Well, that ain't the same thing atall!" he exclaimed, getting angered by all the attention.

More laughter followed, but Adler let the conversation drift, knowing it was best not to get the big man overly hot. Hell, he could take them all apart for sport, limb by limb, in three minutes flat.

"I need a drink," Tony said, catching his breath. His lined face was flushed from laughing. He turned to Earl, who stared at him coldly. "Hey, you got any whiskey around here? Or beer . . . or somethin'?"

"I don't drink," Earl said. "Don't allow it on the premises."

"Well, that's a little extreme," Tony said.

Adler turned to Benji. "Kid, go fetch my saddlebags from the barn."

"What for, Wayne?"

"Just go."

When Benji returned, bursting through the door on a wave of bone-splitting air and snow, he had the saddlebags draped over a shoulder. He heaved the door closed against the wailing tempest and flung the saddlebags on the table. "But gosh, it's windy out there! I think it's lettin' up some, though, Wayne. I seen some stars."

"It'll prob'ly be clear as a bell by mornin'," Tony said hopefully.

"And colder'n a witch's tit," T. J. Cross added.

Adler was rummaging through his saddlebags. "Well, boys, I'd hoped to open this stuff after we made the border, but I guess, under the circumstances, we need it more now." He produced three burlap-wrapped bundles from the saddlebags and removed the burlap until three new bottles of whiskey stood on the table, the brown liquid glowing amber in the lantern light.

"Good Lord . . . you been holdin' out on us, Adler," Cross said, staring at the bottles lasciviously.

"For your own good, T. J., for your own good. You know how you and whiskey sometimes don't mix so well. I was afraid you and Tony'd get into it and do somethin' stupid."

"Fuck you, Wayne," Cross said. "I can hold my whiskey as good as you or anybody else. Now shut up and pour."

"Pour, hell!" Tony exclaimed. "Pass me a bottle."

"Now, now, boys," Adler chided. "If you don't behave yourselves, I'm gonna have Benji take these bottles right back where they came from." He gave Cross and Riemersma a mock-fatherly look of censure. It was all a show and they knew it. Adler was well aware of the men's weakness for liquor, and was exploiting it for his own amusement.

The men stared at him angrily, and he held the stares for about twenty seconds. Finally, he laughed delightedly, uncorked a bottle, and poured several fingers into coffee cups.

"What about you, kid?" he asked Benji.

The giant shook his head quickly. "I-I don't like that stuff, Wayne."

"What about you folks in there?" Wayne said, holding the bottle above his head and regarding his hostages in the living room's shadows.

"No, thanks," Jody said dryly.

"Well . . . all right, then," Wayne said, splashing whiskey into his own cup, a cigarillo wedged in the corner of his mouth. "Just more for us, eh, T.J?"

They'd played for fifteen minutes, smoking and drinking, when Tony leaned toward Adler and said in a hushed voice, "Hey, Wayne. What are we gonna do with them folks?"

Adler spoke loudly enough for everyone to hear. "Well, I don't know, Tony. What do you think we should do with them?"

"They can identify us," T. J. said matter-of-factly, picking a card off the stack and slipping it into his hand.

"T. J. has a point," Wayne said.

Tony looked slightly appalled. "So . . . we're gonna kill 'em? All of 'em?"

"Well, like T. J. pointed out," Wayne said, considering his cards and chewing on his cigar, "they can identify us, Tony. I know it ain't a pleasant thought but, hey, we killed all those soldier boys now, didn't we? If I remember correct, you even shot one in the back as he was runnin' away."

"Yeah, but . . . this is different," Tony said, looking like he'd just eaten something disgusting. "I mean, there's women and a child . . . and one's in the family way."

Cross said, "If we don't kill them, Tony, we'll be runnin' for the rest of our lives. We won't have one minute to stop and enjoy this money. Every sheriff and bounty hunter and federal marshal in the whole damn country will have our pictures memorized and be gunnin' for us. The Canadians will be lookin', too. And we'll never—no way, my friend—make it to Mexico. Not a prayer." He shook ashes from his cigar. "I call your fifteen, Wayne, and raise you the teacher."

"Huh?" Adler said around his cigarillo.

"Miss Beaumont in there. Whoever wins the most money at the end of the night gets her. The losers have to do the dirty work in the morning."

Adler looked at Tony and Benji. Tony's face still betrayed his reluctance, but Benji was grinning. He giggled and covered his mouth. Adler leaned across the table and shook Cross's hand.

"You hear that in there?" Wayne called. "Miss Beaumont just got throwed into the kitty!"

Crystal lifted her head from Fay's lap and dropped her feet to the floor. "Shut your mouths, you slimy, goddamn savages!"

"Crystal, be quiet!" Jody hissed from his rocker.

"What'd you call us?" Cross said angrily.

Crystal opened her mouth to yell again. Fay grabbed her shoulders. "Crystal, don't . . . it'll be all right."

Crystal turned to her, eyes bright with hatred. "Fay—"

"It'll be all right," Fay quietly insisted.

Crystal dropped her voice. "Didn't you hear what they said they were going to do?"

Fay pulled Crystal close and whispered in her ear. "I heard. And I couldn't be more pleased."

Crystal pulled away, shocked. *"What?"*

"You two keep quiet over there, or I'll take a strap to the both of ya's," Adler said, his voice growing thick from drink.

Benji smirked and Tony chuckled.

"They're done talkin'," Jody said, sending a good-natured smile toward the kitchen. "Everything's all right."

Crystal shot him a hard look.

He whispered just audibly, "Crystal, be still!"

Crystal regarded him and Fay like they'd both gone loco.

When the hardcases went back to their card game, Jody went back to work on the cotton strips tethering his wrists. About an hour ago, he'd discovered that one of the slats in the rocker's back was split, offering a cutting edge. The narrow wedge of split wood wasn't as sharp as he would have liked—it kept him busy, minute by minute, sliding the cotton tether across it—but it was the only edge he had, and it was working. So far, he'd gotten halfway through the cloth, and if he could work uninterrupted for another half hour, he thought he'd have it cut through.

What he'd do once he was free, he had no idea—only that, one way or another, he had to get his hands on a gun.

Jody worked at the cloth, trying to keep his shoulders from moving. The wind howled and nettled the cabin's log walls. Occasionally, Candace whispered to her mother. Doreen answered the frightened child soothingly, patting her back.

At one point Jody's chair creaked as he worked with a little too much intensity. Earl looked at him curiously. Jody stopped working at the straps and shot a look into the kitchen. None of the men appeared to have heard. Jody turned to Earl, shook his head once, meaningfully, and continued working.

Ten minutes later the wedge of split wood gave with an audible crack. Jody froze. The men in the kitchen looked around, curious.

"What the hell was that?" Adler said.

"The stove," Jody said, a little too quickly.

"That wasn't no stove," Adler said. "Sounded like wood snappin' to me. Benji, go over and check the half-breed's ties."

"Why do I always gotta—?"

" 'Cause if it weren't for me you'd still be swampin' out saloons in Butte!"

Looking hurt, the big idiot laid his cards down and scraped his chair back. Jody watched him move toward him, his pulse pounding so hard his vision swam. He knew he'd gotten nearly all the way through the cloth. If only he could tear through the rest . . . He inhaled, held his breath, and forced all his strength into his arms and shoulders, doing everything in his power to separate his wrists.

Benji's boots pounded on the puncheon floor. "Hey, what are you up to, anyway?" the giant asked, seeing Jody's flushed face and the sweat beaded on his forehead.

The cloth gave. Jody's wrists sprang free. At the same instant, Jody bounded to his feet and lunged toward the big idiot, who stopped suddenly only three feet away. Before the big man could react, Jody grabbed the gun out of Benji's holster, intending to fling as much lead into the kitchen as possible, hoping to get all three outlaws before they could get him or anyone else in the living room.

As he brought the gun up, Earl sprang out of his chair and into Benji, knocking the big man backward against the wall and out of Jody's way. Jody thumbed back the revolver's trigger and aimed.

But he was too late. T. J. Cross had already stood and cleared leather. His gun barked, spitting smoke and fire. The slug tore through Jody like a hot poker, numbing his shoulder and rendering his right arm useless. He tripped the trigger on Benji's gun, but the shot sailed wild and lodged in a cupboard door.

Everything was a blur after that. Vaguely, he was aware of flying back against the chair and of Crystal screaming his name, his body filling with a white-hot pain.

His brain registered a poignant, ear-ringing sense of defeat and the sudden knowledge that he, Crystal, Fay, Earl, Doreen, and young Candace . . . they were all doomed.

9

STILLMAN AND MCMANNIGLE were between poker hands, and Leon had gotten up to stoke the stove, when the office door suddenly opened. A stout figure in a blue wool coat blew in on a gust of wind and snow that nearly swept the lanterns out.

"Sheriff!" the man cried behind the wool scarf wrapped around his head. "We need you over at the Drovers. Ol' Banner Harlow's shootin' up the place!"

"Harlow?" Stillman said, incredulous. Banner Harlow was a harmless old farmer from north of town. He was a regular at the Drovers Saloon, but Stillman had never known the man to act violently.

"Nah . . . not Banner Harlow," Leon said, echoing Stillman's skepticism.

"Sure enough," said the man, whom Stillman recognized as Louis Cline, the cook out at the Wellman spread. "We was all just sittin' around drinkin' and waitin' out the storm, and then ol' Banner pulls two pistols from his belt, takes aim at the elk head on the wall, and shoots a horn off. Then he starts aimin' at the other heads around the place and at the bottles behind the bar.

Meantime, ever'one's scramblin' this way and that and hidin' behind tables. I was the only one who made it out. Ever'body else is trapped behind the bar."

"You're sure it's Banner?" Stillman asked.

"Sure as shit!"

Stillman turned to Leon. "What in the hell you suppose has gotten into that crazy granger?"

"Must be the storm," Leon speculated. "Some men just go plumb weak north of their ears during a storm. Crazy as sheepherders."

"Either that or Elmer Burk's lacing his rye with strychnine," Stillman said, buttoning his coat. "Louis, you stay here and keep the stoves stoked, will you?"

"My pleasure, Sheriff."

"Ready?" Stillman asked Leon, heading for the door.

"Yeah, I'm ready," the deputy grumbled. "Ready to curl up with Rachel over at Mrs. Lee's."

They turned their collars up and headed outside, turning east on First Street, fighting their way through the snowdrifts on their way to Second Avenue.

The sun had gone down hours ago, but the snow emanated enough light for Stillman to make out the vague forms of the buildings lining First. He and Leon trudged through the drifts that were sometimes nearly as high as their waists, squinting their eyes against the penetrating cold and the pelting flakes. Occasionally, Stillman turned around to make sure Leon was behind him and they didn't get separated. Even in town, a blizzard like this could disorient a person, the snow blinding them, the wind sucking the air from their lungs, and get them wandering in circles until they collapsed, exhausted, in a drift.

When they came to the barbershop on the corner of First Street and turned down Second Avenue, Stillman tripped over the boardwalk, which was completely buried in snow. The powder was so deep he couldn't find a purchase, and Leon ran up to give him a hand.

"This is goddamn ridiculous," Stillman complained, but the roaring wind tore the words from his lips.

He'd meant it was ridiculous for anyone to shoot up a saloon in a blizzard. Wasn't the storm bad enough? He still wasn't convinced the shooter was Banner Harlow, the mild-mannered granger who drove to town with his wife every Saturday to shop and to gas with the loafers in the mercantiles. Harlow often stopped at the Drovers for a glass of beer, but Stillman couldn't imagine the man shooting up the place. Hell, he couldn't remember ever seeing the farmer wearing a gun.

He and McMannigle had walked another hard-fought block when they started hearing sporadic gunfire. Halting on the boardwalk a half block down from the Drovers, Stillman pulled his Colt out from under his coat. Leon did likewise. They shared a dark look, then proceeded toward the Drovers. When they came to the building's corner, Stillman turned to Leon.

He had to yell above the wind. "Why don't you go around back? I'll take the front."

Leon nodded, clutching his hat to his head, and trudged through the snow between the saloon and the dry-goods next door. Stillman watched him, wincing against the wind sluicing under the awning.

When McMannigle was only a dim outline in the blowing snow, Stillman ducked under the Drovers' plate-glass window, noting the three bullet holes in the glass, and made his way to the door.

Inside, a man yelled. A gun barked. A woman screamed.

"Goddamnit," Stillman grumbled, crouching with his back to the building.

Turning to the door, he saw that the glass in the upper

half had been entirely shot out. There were two bullet holes in the wood directly below. The gun roared again, and the crash of breaking glass sounded.

Keeping his head below the broken-out window, Stillman tripped the latch and threw the door wide. Stepping back behind the front of the building, he looked through the open door, quickly raking his eyes across the room, which was lit by oil lamps, the only things that, oddly, hadn't been a target.

Sure enough, old Banner sat at a table against the wall, wielding a six-shooter. A bottle, a whiskey tumbler, and another revolver sat before him. His face was gaunt and whiskered. He wore a red-checked mackinaw and a black wool cap. Wisps of gray hair stuck out from under the cap. Lifting the gun in his hand, Harlow was about to take aim at something across the room when he spied Stillman. Turning toward the sheriff, he sent a bullet Stillman's way.

The bullet careened out the open door and lodged in an awning post, and a woman cried from behind the bar, "Stop it, you crazy old coot!"

Stillman yelled, "Goddamnit, Banner . . . what the hell do you think you're doin'?"

"Shootin' up the place—and why the hell not?" the old man hoarsely replied. He followed up the yell with another pistol report. A bottle behind the bar exploded, and the woman screamed again.

The man had indeed gone crazy. Stillman had seen it before; he just hadn't expected it to happen to the quiet Banner Harlow, who'd never had a harsh word for anyone.

"Ben, you out there?" a man yelled from behind the bar. Stillman recognized the voice of the Drovers' proprietor, Elmer Burk.

"I'm here, Elmer. Just stay put. Everything will be all right."

"All right? Hell, that old bastard's gone plumb loco. Look what he's done to my place!"

The old man cackled and fired a round into the bar.

"Goddamn him to hell!" Elmer Burk cried. "He's gonna kill all of us!"

"You and the others just stay put," Stillman said. He shifted his eyes to Banner Harlow, who sat at the table tipping back the tumbler. "Toss that gun on the floor, Banner."

Harlow set the tumbler down. "I ain't gonna do that, Sheriff."

"Banner, what's gotten into you?"

"I'm drunk and crazy, Sheriff. You're gonna have to kill me."

"I don't want to kill you, Banner. You're a good man."

"Not no more I'm not." He lifted the revolver, aimed it in Stillman's general direction, and squeezed off a shot.

It was obvious he wasn't trying to hit anyone. Apparently, he was trying to provoke Stillman into killing him, which the sheriff could easily do. Sitting there all alone against the wall, Harlow presented an easy target. But gunning down Banner Harlow was the last thing Stillman wanted to do.

He couldn't fathom why a quiet, hardworking man like Banner Harlow would suddenly become suicidal. He'd seen it in less well-balanced men who had lost another in a long line of jobs or whose women had left them. But as far as Stillman knew, Harlow's farm was doing well, and Stillman couldn't imagine Harlow's wife, a female version of the farmer himself—level-headed, hardworking—leaving Harlow for another man.

The only thing Stillman knew for sure was that he had to subdue the man before he inadvertently killed someone with a ricochet.

He took a minute to come up with a plan to apprehend old Harlow without getting the farmer or anyone else hurt, then waited for another report from Harlow's gun. He didn't have to wait long. Before the echo had died in the smoky room, he bolted through the open door. Crouching behind tables, he moved behind the faro table and tipped it over, using its surface for a shield.

"I'm not gonna tell you again, Banner—drop those guns!"

"Won't do it, Sheriff," the old man bellowed. The gun roared, and the round punched into Stillman's table, which was, fortunately, solid oak.

"If you don't drop those weapons and stand with your hands up, Harlow, I'm gonna have to plug you."

"Do what you have to, Sheriff!" Another report followed the exclamation.

Stillman peeked around the corner of his table. The room was so smoky he could barely see the old man, sitting about twenty feet away, back stiff, head lolling, arms on the table. He made no move to shield himself from Stillman's fire. He was either too inebriated to care, or he wanted to die.

Stillman glanced around the room. McMannigle peered around the craps table near the back door, gun in hand. Shifting his gaze back to Harlow, Stillman saw that the man was reloading one of his guns. Stillman considered storming him, but what if the other gun wasn't empty?

Stillman looked at McMannigle, caught the deputy's eye, and held up six fingers. Leon nodded, and slid back behind the table.

Stillman said to Harlow, "Throw it down now, Banner. You don't want to die."

Harlow slammed the magazine door closed and spun the cylinder. He loosed a shot at Stillman's table.

"Everybody in this here room's gonna die if I don't, Sheriff." He fired again at the wall behind the bar, shattering another bottle.

"Goddamn you to hell, Banner!" Elmer Burk yelled.

Stillman lifted his gun and fired a bullet over the old man's shoulder. Harlow instinctively flinched, but immediately regained his stoic, devil-may-care composure. "You're a little off to the right, Sheriff."

He took another shot at Stillman's table, smoke puffing around his head, the slug plowing into the oak, the hollow crack rattling Stillman's eardrums.

"You're not doing much better, Banner."

"Never was much of a shot," the farmer said, shooting another round into Stillman's table.

That's four shots, Stillman thought. Only two more . . .

"Maybe you really don't want to hurt anyone, Banner."

"Come out from behind that table an' see if I don't," Harlow called. He blew another widget of oak from Stillman's hardwood shield.

One more . . .

Stillman waited, hearing the wind blow through the open doors, feeling the chill penetrate the smoky room. Snow powdered the floor.

Come on, Banner, he thought. Shoot your last shot.

Finally, Stillman peered around the table, bringing up his Colt. He fired a slug so close to the old farmer's right ear that Harlow, flinching, almost fell out of his chair. Angrily, he raised his gun at Stillman and loosed the last shot in his gun.

Stillman ducked behind the table as the lead flew wild, then scrambled to his feet yelling, "Go, Leon . . . grab him!"

Standing, Stillman stretched his gun hand straight out in front of him and sighted down the seven-and-a-half-inch barrel at the revolver lying on Harlow's table. The six-shooter was a good foot to the right of the farmer's hand, with the wall directly behind it. Stillman thought he had at least an eighty-percent chance of hitting the gun without pinking Banner.

Just before Banner's hand fell on the six-shooter, Stillman's slug flung it off the table with a metallic bark and clatter.

"No!" Banner cried.

McMannigle ran toward him from across the room. Stillman did likewise, shoving tables out of his way.

Leon reached the farmer just as he bent to retrieve the revolver. The deputy dove on the man and flung him to the floor. Wailing and crying, Banner got a hand on the gun and brought it up. Stillman kicked it out of his hand. It sailed ten feet and slid another fifteen.

"It's over, Banner," Stillman said to the old farmer struggling feebly on the floor with Leon.

The old man gave up and relaxed his body. "Damn ye . . . damn ye, anyway, Sheriff," he grumbled.

Leon climbed to his feet. Stillman looked behind the bar. "It's all right, Elmer. It's all over. We have him."

Singly and in pairs, the people who'd been hiding behind the bar stood up, brushing themselves off and looking harried, wide-eyed with trepidation. They were four cowboys in mackinaws and Stetsons, a pleasure girl named Lana, and Elmer Burk, a slender man with short gray hair, a waxed, salt-and-pepper mustache, and an apron.

Burk looked angrily around the room. "Goddamnit!"

he fumed. "Look what that son of a bitch done to my place!"

"What set him off?" Leon asked, donning his black Stetson. Banner Harlow lay on his side, on the floor. He looked dead, though his eyes were open.

"He just started shootin', Deputy," one of the drovers said timidly. "Drank half a bottle o' whiskey in about five minutes, pulled those pistols, and just started shootin' around the room, startin' with the elk head up yonder."

"Why, we were trapped in here!" Lana said, scowling and grabbing her bare shoulders. With the doors open, it was nearly as cold in the saloon as it was outside. The wood stoves had long gone out.

"Better go upstairs and get some clothes on, Lana," Stillman advised. He turned to the bartender. "Sorry about the mess, Burk. I'm sure these men will help you get the door and windows boarded up." He shifted his gaze to Leon. "You want to give them a hand?"

"You bet."

"I'll take ol' Banner over to the jailhouse and try to find out what's twisted his tail."

"Lock up his sorry ass!" Burk roared, walking out from behind the bar to assess the damage.

Stillman helped the old farmer to his feet. He half-dragged him to the door, outside, and across the street, fighting the snow and wind. They pushed through the office door on a gale shoving them from behind.

Seeing them, Louis Cline jumped out of Stillman's swivel chair behind the desk, where he'd been playing solitaire. The stove was roaring and the room was toasty. Louis didn't say anything, just stared disdainfully at the hang-headed Banner Harlow.

"Sit down in front of my desk, Banner," Stillman ordered. "Louis, why don't you help Leon and the others over at the Drovers?"

"Sure thing, Sheriff."

When he'd left, Stillman took off his coat, hat, and gloves, and hung them on the pegs by the door. He went to the stove and poured two cups of coffee, one of which he set on his desk in front of the inert Banner Harlow. He sipped from the other one and hiked a hip on the corner of his desk.

"Okay, spill it, Banner," Stillman said with a sigh. "What the hell got into you?"

For a whole minute it was as though Banner hadn't heard the question. Then, slowly, he lifted his head and raked air into his lungs, his drunk-rheumy eyes gazing unseeing at the far wall.

"I-I took a rope out to the barn . . . but I couldn't do it. . . ."

Stillman's brows furrowed. "Hang yourself?"

The wizened old man, looking like a scarecrow in his oversized mackinaw, nodded almost imperceptibly.

"Why?"

Banner turned his head and inclined it slightly to stare into Stillman's befuddled eyes. "She's dead."

Stillman scowled. "Who's dead?"

"Mary," the old man said softly, distractedly, his mind only partly in the present. Stillman knew that Mary was Harlow's wife, and she often accompanied Banner to town on Saturdays.

Stillman lowered his head and ran a hand through his hair. "I didn't know Mary passed away, Banner."

The old man nodded. "Yep . . . she's gone." He looked away.

"When?"

"This mornin' . . . before the storm hit. I went inside after chores for breakfast, and I knew somethin' was wrong 'cause all the bacon was fried up to little black slivers." Tears glazed his eyes, and Stillman waited for him to continue. "I called around for her . . . then I went into the bedroom, and there she was. Just lyin' there in her dress and apron." Another pause. He brushed the back of his mitten against his cheek. "She musta got to feelin' poorly and went to lay down. . . ."

Stillman looked at the floor, his ears ringing with sadness for the man. He didn't say anything, and neither did Harlow. The fire in the stove cracked and popped and the wind battered the little office mercilessly, the drafts shunting the flames in the lanterns.

Finally the old man looked at Stillman, his gaunt face contorted with grief. "Couldn't . . . couldn't you just put a bullet in my head, Sheriff?" The old man sobbed; it was almost a wail. "You have a woman . . . you don't know what it's like. . . . Fifty year we were together, Mary and me. We buried two kids, two run off, and it's just been her and me these last twenty year . . . Mary and me."

Banner Harlow dropped his head on the table and sobbed like a child.

Stillman sat there stony-faced, his heart tearing. He felt like crying for the old man, wondering at the harshness of life. He knew that if anything happened to Fay he'd yearn for a bullet as intensely as Banner Harlow yearned for one now.

Stillman stood and squeezed the old man's shoulder. After a while, he walked over to the window and stared out at the storm.

Fay . . .

10

CRYSTAL HAD SEEN the shooting as though it had happened in a slow dream—Jody bolting from his chair and grabbing the big man's gun, the man called T. J. throwing his chair back as he stood and drawing his own weapon, lifting it to his shoulder, and firing. Jody flying back against his chair, rolling onto the floor, and grabbing his shoulder in agony.

"No!" Crystal screamed. "Jody!" In a second, she was kneeling beside him.

Adler's voice was a whip. "Get away from him, goddamnit!"

Crystal's hand came away from Jody's shoulder, soaked in blood. "Jody . . . my God . . . don't die . . . please don't die." Her voice was thin. She sobbed.

"Crystal," Jody said, through teeth gritted in pain. "It's okay . . . get away from me." His eyes were on Adler, approaching with his cocked revolver held down at his side. The man's eyes had emptied and his mouth was a straight slash across his face.

His voice had acquired a tense, breathy timbre. "I said get away from him, unless you want it, too!"

Crystal turned, enraged. "Leave him alone!" she screamed. "You *bastard* . . . leave him alone . . . !"

Heavy as she was with child, Crystal bolted to her feet and went at Adler with both fists swinging, face flushed with fury. She slugged the man's face several times before he got his left arm up to ward her off. She swung with her right, then with her left, then with her right, each time connecting only with the man's arm. It was like hitting a bale of hay. Her knuckles cracked and her wrists ached, but the pain didn't stop her. Between blows, Crystal saw that Adler's expression had changed from anger to wide-eyed amusement. He even laughed.

Incensed at his mockery, she swung another right, harder this time, but again only connected with his arm. Before she could wind up again, someone grabbed her from behind. It was Fay.

"Crystal, no . . . honey . . . stop."

"Crystal, goddamnit!" Jody ordered, his voice sharp with pain. "Sit down!"

Physically and mentally exhausted, Crystal collapsed in Fay's arms. She sank to the floor crying. "You bastard . . . I hate you, I hate you," she said to Adler.

Wayne was laughing as though it was the funniest joke he'd ever heard in his life, bent over and slapping his thighs. Standing at the table, where he'd watched the shooting and Crystal's attack on Adler, Tony Riemersma laughed as well, but with less abandon than Adler. He appeared tense and vaguely puzzled by the recent events. He hadn't expected the storm, to be stranded here with these people, whom he was going to have to help kill. Riemersma was not by nature a violent man. He'd killed only one man before today, and that had been a bank guard bearing down on him with a shotgun. He was just an ordinary safecracker who now suddenly felt as though he'd been thrown into a wolf pack.

T. J. Cross was not laughing. He wasn't even smiling. Seeing that Adler was on the prod, he stepped into the sitting room, making a slow beeline for Jody, his gun held down before his thigh, a dark, savage look in his glassy eyes.

Fay saw him, and her heart beat fiercely. "Don't . . . don't do this," she pleaded.

Cross kept coming, slowly and deliberately, eyes riveted on Jody, who lay on the floor holding his bleeding shoulder. Cross stopped and raised the revolver, thumbing back the hammer.

"No," Adler said, putting his hand on Cross's arm. "Let him go." He was still laughing, obviously still tickled, but the laughter was losing its intensity. "His little woman saved his hide . . . for now, anyway."

"I'm gonna put a bullet in his idiot head," Cross insisted.

"No, T. J.," Adler said, another laugh escaping his smirking lips. "Did you see her? I love a woman with spunk." Adler slapped his thigh again and guffawed. "Benji, did you see her?"

Benji was standing by the wood stove, looking at Cross with a troubled expression on his big, red-mottled face. "I seen her, Wayne."

Cross said, "I'm gonna shoot him, Wayne. What if he tries that shit again?"

"In his condition? Hell, he'll probably bleed to death in an hour. No, leave him be. That pregnant minx of his deserves it." Adler looked at Crystal, eyes bright with glee. "Honey, I wish you were my wife. I like a woman with spunk. I bet you even like your lovin' a little rough, don't you?"

Sitting at Fay's feet, Crystal stifled a sob and wiped the tears from her tear-swollen face with her hand. "I hope you burn in hell," she hissed.

Adler chuckled. "I'd give you a try if you weren't so heavy with that half-breed's bambino. Hell, I might give you a try later, anyway. . . ." He looked at Earl, who sat against the wall with his hands still tied behind his back, staring at Adler with mute rage.

"You try anything like that again," Wayne said to Earl, "you're going to get the same thing he got, only worse. Benji, put him back in his rocker and tie him to it."

"Right away, Wayne," Benji said. He kicked Earl's hip. "You knocked me down, mister. I don't stand for bein' knocked down by no one."

"You tell him, Benji," Adler mocked as he turned around and headed back to the kitchen table.

Reluctantly, stiffly, like a parent leaving a room of misbehaving children, Cross followed him. The two men sat down and refilled their cups. Cross picked up the cards and riffled them sourly.

Earl pushed himself against the wall, gaining his feet. Breathing heavily from the effort, he said, "Sorry, Jody. You almost had them."

Jody was lying where he'd fallen. Blood seeped through the hand he held to his right shoulder. "Wasn't your fault, Earl. I was just too damn slow, that's all."

"You get over there and sit down," Benji ordered Earl, like a boy playing make-believe. "You want me to break your legs, I will."

Earl scowled at the big man, but did as he said.

Crystal and Fay crouched over Jody, both women trying to contain their alarm.

Crystal peeled Jody's hand from the wound. "Let me see," she said.

"I'm sorry, Crystal," Jody said, swallowing, gazing up into his wife's haunted eyes. "I thought I had a shot."

"How does it look?" Fay said.

Crystal's voice was thin. "Not good. He's losing a lot of blood."

"Just stuff somethin' in there to slow the flow," Jody said lightly. "I'll be all right."

Fay tore off a long strip of material from one of her petticoats and handed it to Crystal. Crystal wadded it up in her hand, and pressed it to the wound. Jody gave a start and grunted with pain.

"Sorry, honey," Crystal said. She smiled at him tenderly, inclining her head slightly. Tears veiled her eyes once again, and a sob escaped her lips.

Jody placed his left hand on the hand she held on his wound. He squeezed and gazed back at her, this young woman he'd known since they were kids, riding horses together in the Two Bears. This woman who carried their child in her womb. "Don't you worry . . . we'll get out of this somehow."

Crystal sobbed again, lowered her head with defeat. Jody gave her hand another squeeze and turned to Fay. "I don't . . . I don't suppose there's any chance Ben'll come looking for you. . . ."

Fay shook her head. "I'm sure he thinks I'm safe." She snorted a dry laugh. "Why wouldn't I be? Besides, he'd never make it in this weather."

Jody swallowed, wincing at a sudden pain. "I thought I saw some stars a while ago. It could be lightening some."

Fay lifted her head to look out the window. She thought she could see a faint star shine, which meant the clouds were thinning. "In that case, he might come with a sleigh . . . in the morning."

"The morning will be too late," Crystal said.

Cross's voice boomed. "Hey, will you folks be quiet in there? I don't want no talkin'. And shut that kid up—I'm tired of hearing her squeal."

Fay looked at Candace. The girl and her mother were sitting on the floor now, before the wood stove, their backs against the settee. Candace sobbed against Doreen's breast. Doreen lifted her head angrily to the men in the kitchen. "She's just a child, and you've frightened her crazy with all your carryin' on!" Her voice broke and she lowered her cheek to Candace's head and wept.

Adler hooted. "We frightened her with all our carryin' on. Hey, look at the teats on that one, Benj." He showed Benji the back of a four of diamonds.

"It's all right," Fay whispered to Candace, whose face was buried in her mother's bosom. The child's back shook as she sobbed, more frightened, Fay supposed, than she'd ever been. This was no doubt the child's worst nightmare.

Fay reached out and placed a hand on the child's back. "We're all going to be just fine, Candace. I promise."

Candace lifted her head and turned her swollen, tear-streaked face to Fay. "No, we aren't, Mrs. Stillman. Those men are gonna kill us all in the morning. I heard 'em say it, I heard 'em." Her voice was shrill with horror, but the men in the kitchen were arguing loudly at the moment over whose turn it was to deal.

Fay looked deeply into the child's large, brown eyes, the rims of which were swollen and red. "I promise you, Candace, we are all going to get out of this alive. Have you ever known me to go back on my word? Have you?"

Candace's meek gaze retreated to the floor. She shook her head.

Fay looked at Doreen, who returned her gaze with a worried, questioning one of her own. "I promise, Doreen," Fay said.

The woman's gaze strayed to her husband. Fay turned to Earl, who looked at her frowning. "How?" he said.

He'd obviously come close to giving up hope himself.

"Hey, what'd I tell you in there!" Cross bellowed hoarsely, slamming his cup down.

"Sorry," Fay said. "It's my fault. We were talking about getting Jody up on the settee, where he'd be more comfortable."

"I don't want the half-breed to be comfortable," Cross said, lips and mustache curling back from his small, square teeth. "I want him to die, nice and slow, right there on the floor."

"You animal," Crystal hissed through gritted teeth.

Fay and Jody admonished her to keep quiet.

"Yeah, that's right, I'm an animal," Cross said. "And your friend, the teacher there, is gonna find out just what kind of an animal I am." He grinned.

"Hey, bullshit, T. J.!" Adler drunkenly objected. "You only got twenty bucks on me, and I'm fixin' to win it back."

"It's almost midnight, my friend," Cross jeered. "At the strike of twelve, whoever's got the biggest kitty gets the teacher."

"You got forty minutes, slick," Adler said.

"No," Cross said, turning his lusty gaze to Fay. "She does."

Candace turned to Fay, her face twisted with sorrow and terror. "Oh, Mrs. Stillman . . ."

Fay patted the child's hand and tried a smile. "It's all right, Candace," she said. "You just remember what I promised."

She looked at Crystal and Jody, both regarding her anxiously. "Wh-what are you gonna do, Fay?" Jody whispered.

Fay didn't have an answer to that question. She had a vague idea about what she was going to try to do, but she hadn't ironed out her plan. She just looked at Jody and smiled reassuringly, hoping he couldn't see the fear she felt deep within her bones.

What she wouldn't give to be in Ben's arms right now. . . .

Ten minutes passed. Crystal tended Jody, Doreen held Candace, and Earl stared grimly at the floor, his features not betraying the discomfort he must have felt with his hands tied snugly to the chair behind him. Fay glanced out the windows, where the star shine appeared to grow more intense. Apparently the snow had stopped.

"Well . . . I'll tell you one goddamn thing . . . I'm hungry," Adler said.

"Me, too, Wayne," Benji said.

Tony shuffled the cards and regarded Benji with his drink-rheumy eyes. "You're always hungry."

"Hey, we want some food in here, Dor-een," Adler said, drawing out the woman's name condescendingly. He slid back his chair, kicked his legs out in front of him, and laced his hands over his belly.

"No," Fay said. "I'll go."

"Yeah . . . come on, teacher," Cross growled. "Come in here and cook, and let me get a look at you."

It was obvious all the men, except Benji, were drunk and getting amorous. It was probably the most danger-ous time in the whole ordeal, Fay knew, and she'd have to tread lightly. It was also an opportune time, however. For what, she wasn't sure, but she hoped to find out soon.

With an inaudible sigh and a bracing smile for the other captives, she stood and walked into the kitchen.

11

AT THE NELSON place, Dr. Evans was making the best of a bad situation.

When he'd finished cleaning his medical tools at the kitchen well pump, he wasted little time in taking a lantern and making a beeline for Nils Nelson's study. It was a low-ceilinged room bedecked with hunting trophies and rough, hand-hewn furniture covered with animal hides. Against one wall sat a hulking, leather-upholstered desk flanked by a framed map of Montana Territory.

Against the wall opposite stood a broad pine cabinet nearly as tall as Evans, who set the lantern on the desk and walked hungrily to the cabinet, rubbing his hands together and grinning.

"Please don't let it be locked," he said aloud, imagining himself following the rope that led to the bunkhouse and asking Ned Nelson about the key.

The doctor stuck his fingers through the wood handles and, holding his breath, pulled. The doors opened, wafting the faint smell of pine resin, molasses, and wine.

"Thank you." Evans inhaled deeply as his gaze rolled

over the finest selection of drinking matter he'd seen in many a year.

He stood reading the labels, until his thirst got the better of him and his right hand wrapped itself around the stout neck of a fine ruby port. From the upper shelf he selected a small green goblet. Cradling the port like a baby in one arm, holding the goblet lightly in the other hand, he headed back to the sitting room, where a fire popped in the massive stone hearth, below the blocky black head of a snarling grizzly.

He set the bottle and goblet on the wide arm of an overstuffed leather chair, angled before the fire. From his medical bag he retrieved the Keats he'd been trying to read this afternoon, settled into the chair, opened the port, and filled the green goblet all the way to the rim. He held the tumbler up to the firelight, admiring the rich vermilion glow through the thick green glass, sighed pleasurably, said, "Go with God, Clyde, go with God," and brought the sultry liquid to his lips. He held the port in his mouth, swishing it around, and swallowed, feeling the fire spread down his throat, through his belly, and deep into his loins.

"Ahhh . . ."

"Clyde."

The voice clawed at him like nails on slate. He turned in his chair to see Katherine Kemmet descending the open stairs. "What is it?"

"Where's Ned?"

"He went out to the bunkhouse. Now if you wouldn't mind, I'm having a nip."

"I do mind, Clyde," she said, approaching his chair, eyebrows raised like a schoolmarm. "I'm going to be needing a little help, I'm afraid."

He frowned. It was really more of a sneer. "Help?"

"Yes, with the bed linen. It needs to be changed, and since Ned isn't here, you'll have to help me move Mrs. Nelson and the baby into another room."

"Oh, for crying out . . . I'll call Ned."

"Oh, no, you won't call that poor boy out in this storm. It'll just take a minute." She took the goblet out of his hand and set it on the mantel. "Come, come," she said, irritatingly cheery, and headed for the stairs.

Certain that the chore was something she'd concocted to keep him from his pleasure, Evans sat fuming, hands clenched on the chair's armrests.

"Clyde," Katherine called again, with an admonishing edge.

Evans turned. She was standing at the bottom of the stairs, one hand on the banister, regarding him derisively.

"Goddamnit," he grumbled, pushing himself out of the chair. "Katherine, you are a genuine pain in the—"

"Now, Clyde! Don't you go unleashing your lewd tongue in the home of this good Christian family and their newborn babe!"

Grudgingly, he followed her up the stairs and into Mrs. Nelson's bedroom, feeling the warmth of that first drink dissipate under his anger.

"Alice, I'm going to have the doctor lift you into another bed while I change your sheets, all right?"

In the glow of a single lantern, the young woman appeared washed out and fatigued, but she nodded and formed a smile. She was the daughter of a neighboring rancher, and Evans thought she was about twenty years old. Nils Nelson, who was old enough to be her grandfather, had started courting her the year after his wife died. She was pretty in an unsophisticated, hardworking sort of way. Her hair was a nest of loose blond curls about her head and neck.

"Well, Clyde?" Katherine said as she lifted the baby from its mother's arms.

"Oh . . . yeah, well . . . here we go," Evans grumbled, bending down and shoving one hand under Alice's neck, the other under her knees. He lifted with a grunt, straightened, and headed for the door.

"Just across the hall will be fine, Doctor," Alice said. "That's Ned's and Cal's old room. Poor Ned—Nils makes him sleep in the bunkhouse now, but he's just a boy."

"Well, I suppose it's one way of teaching him the ropes," Evans said conversationally.

The door on the other side of the dark hall was ajar. He kicked it open and stepped inside. It was a small room with a coal heater and an iron bed sagging in the middle. An old muzzle-loader rifle hung on a wall, and rough wooden toys lay atop a dresser. Katherine had already lighted a lantern.

"That's fine—thank you, Doctor," Alice said as he deposited her on the bed. "I hope I wasn't too heavy."

"Light as a feather," Evans said.

Katherine came in behind him and handed the baby to Alice. "Do you have a family, Dr. Evans?" Alice asked as, with no embarrassment at all, she slid the strap of her nightie down her arm, revealing her full left breast. She held the baby to the breast, and it immediately started to suckle.

"No, I'm a bachelor," Evans said, glancing sheepishly off. He'd delivered his share of babies, but the intimacy between mother and child still made him uncomfortable, and he never liked to linger during such moments.

"That's a shame, Doctor. Perhaps you'll marry one day."

Evans gave a patronizing smile. "I doubt it." He started toward the door. Her voice drew him back.

"But why?"

"Well," Evans said, growing even more uncomfortable, glancing nervously around the room, "because I . . . I . . . don't want to." He smiled the patronizing smile again, and again turned to leave. He made it as far as the door.

"Mrs. Kemmet is a widow," young Alice said innocently. "Perhaps you two should think about—"

"Ah, I don't think that . . . ah . . . that Mrs. Kemmet and I would make a . . . the . . . the, uh . . . kind of matched pair one would normally expect of a healthy twosome," Evans hurried to point out, feeling his face grow hot.

He glanced at Katherine, who stood beside the bed, hands folded before her and looking quite pleased with his discomfort.

"Oh, really, Clyde?" she said mockingly. "How do you know? We might make a charming couple!"

"I think this is neither the place nor the time," Evans said, growing angry. "Perhaps you'd better get that linen changed, so Mrs. Nelson here can get back into the comfort of her own bed."

"I'm sorry—I didn't mean to embarrass you, Dr. Evans," Alice said. "I'm just so happy with this little one here—Little Karla—and I know Nils will be, too, when he gets home. . . ."

"I'm sure you are," Evans said, feeling plucky, more than a little offended by the girl's innocent presumption. "I know it's probably hard for you to understand this, Mrs. Nelson, but not everyone in the world finds fulfillment in the pleasing of wives and the rearing of children, who, I've often found, grow up to be little more than. . . ." Seeing the expression on the young woman's face, as well as on Katherine's, Evans decided to let the sentence die on his lips, unfinished.

"Well, anyway," he said, gesturing to the door. "Shall we, Katherine?"

She passed him on her way out the door, looking none too pleased with his behavior. He muttered a curse under his breath and started down the hall toward the stairs.

"Where are you going, Clyde?" she said. "I could use some help with the linen . . . if it's not too much bother, of course?" Her voice was frigid.

"Well, actually, it is, Katherine. My father didn't spend a good year of his salary putting me through medical school just so I could help a midwife change bed linen."

"What a pathetic thing you are, Clyde. A slave to that drink downstairs."

The barb hit its mark; it was as though he'd been tapped behind both knees. It made him feel even more defensive, even more angry. Who were these women to castigate him? "I'm not a slave to anything, goddamnit!"

"Yes, you are," Katherine said, planting a fist on each hip and holding her ground. "Why, you can't wait to get your hands on that drink you poured! You're so feverish for it that you won't even do me the decency of helping me change the linen on Alice's bed!"

"The reason I won't help you change the linen, Katherine," he returned, face red with outrage, "is because it's not my job and because you think you can order me around like some hired plowboy! You forget that I'm the doctor—I'm the professional here. You're the midwife!"

"Oh!" she cried, turning into the room and slamming the door.

Fuming, Evans headed downstairs, muttering to himself angrily. On the first landing he stopped. From out of nowhere he was blind by an enormous wave of guilt. It was a totally foreign feeling. He hadn't remembered feeling guilty since he'd denied his father's wish that he practice with his brothers in New York, instead going West—fifteen years ago! He sure as hell had never felt guilty about anything he'd done or hadn't done in the way of women.

Evans was a totally egocentric person. He knew it and congratulated himself for it. To him it meant that he lived his life on the outside the way he felt it on the inside. It made him that rare bird—a truly honest person. What you saw was what you got.

But now he knew that if he continued downstairs and got snugged back down in his chair, he wouldn't be able to enjoy it. He knew that because he'd be thinking of Katherine upstairs changing the bed linen by herself—as befitted her status—the lovely ruby port would go down like coal oil.

"Oh, for the love of God!" he grumbled, as furious with himself as with her.

He wheeled and walked slowly back up the stairs, one exaggerated step at a time.

12

AS FAY SLICED potatoes into a hot skillet, she heard the snickers and felt the raking eyes of the men sitting at the table behind her. Adler whispered something and Benji laughed through his hands. Adler whispered again.

"Wa-ayne!" Benji cajoled, loving their naughty fun.

The others roared.

Fay felt a slight tug on her skirt. She turned to see Adler snapping his arm back and looking coy. "Please don't do that," she said, feeling as humiliated as she'd ever felt in her life. She was angry enough to slam the iron skillet against Adler's head.

All in good time, she told herself. All in good time.

"I didn't do nothin'!" Adler said.

"You boys think you're real funny, don't you?" Earl grumbled from his chair.

"It's all right, Earl," Fay said. "Please . . . let's just . . . remain calm."

"Yeah, keep your pants on, Earl," T. J. said. He was leaned back like a man waiting for a train, one hand wrapped around his whiskey cup, the other arm resting on the back of his chair. He was gazing at Fay snakily, amused. Pleasantly contemplative.

When Fay had the potatoes frying in the pan, she sliced the remaining meat off the roast Doreen had cooked earlier. She cut open several remaining biscuits, swabbed each with butter, and made sandwiches. She set the sandwiches on a plate and set the plate before the men waiting at the table, watching her lewdly as they smoked and drank.

Adler reached for a biscuit. "I have potatoes and gravy coming," she said.

"Bring it on, beautiful," Adler said.

"Hey, watch your tongue, Adler," T. J. said jokingly. "She's mine. I won her fair and square, and just as soon as my belly's filled, I'm gonna take her into Ma and Pa Hawley's bedroom. Might even take her to Canada with me. Marry her up in Calgary."

"Hey, shut up!" Tony admonished Cross, frowning.

"Shut up yourself, Tony," Cross returned. "It don't matter what they hear, 'cause they ain't gonna be around to tell anyone after the storm, anyways."

"I can kill 'em for ya right now if ya want me to, T. J.," Benji said, boyishly seeking approval. "Real quietlike."

"Not yet, Benji," Cross said. He wanted to postpone any killing for as long as possible. For one thing, he didn't want the mess. For another, his sadistic bent wanted the hostages alive so he could play with them. Staring at Tony, the old safecracker, whose haunted eyes fell to the table, he said, "You feelin' squeamish about what we're gonna have to do before we leave here?"

Old Tony didn't answer for about fifteen seconds. He lifted his eyes, his forehead creased with apprehension. "Well . . . I guess I am feelin' a little troubled at the thought of killin' these people, T. J.," he said reasonably.

"I mean, they're good, hardworkin' folks, and the young lady in there . . . why . . . she's in the family way. Killing a girl in the family way is . . . well, that's an awful thing."

He shuttled his gaze to Adler, fishing for support.

Adler was a firebrand—there was no doubt of that—but he wasn't as cold-blooded a killer as T. J., who was known to coerce men into gunfights just for fun, and leave them chest-shot in dark alleys. He'd killed whores, as well, beating them with his fists or with his belt. Tony had a feeling such a death was going to be the end of Miss Beaumont; he just hoped it wouldn't be the end of the young blonde and the little girl. While killing any woman was against Riemersma's unconscious code of ethics, his gut did flip-flops when he thought of killing a pregnant woman and a child. He knew there was little he could do to prevent it; he just hoped he'd have as little to do with the grisly task as possible.

He could see in Adler's face, however, that he wasn't going to get the kind of backing he'd been hoping for. The man's eyes were dark behind a thin, alcoholic sheen of lunacy.

"Well, what do you suppose we do with them, Tony?" Adler asked.

"Can't we . . . can't we . . . well, I don't know, Wayne. But, I just . . . I don't know—I just can't see mysel—"

"So what you're sayin' then is we—Benji, T. J., and me—we should do the dirty work for you."

"No, I mean—"

"Hey," Cross interrupted. "We had a deal. I get the teacher here—me and her, together, in the other room, *comprende*? You three can do whatever you want with these folks down here, and after the storm you have to get rid of whoever's still kickin'." He smiled at Fay, who was nervously stirring the potatoes and trying not to listen to the conversation. "Which may or may not include the teacher."

Tony picked at a callus on his thumb and gave a troubled sigh. He looked into the shadows of the sitting room, where Doreen and Candace sat together on the floor, staring back at Tony and the other outlaws wide-eyed. He looked at Earl, hunched over in his chair, hands behind his back, and at Crystal, holding a bandage over Jody's wound and whispering into the young man's ear.

Old Riemersma felt a keen injustice; he knew Cross would just as soon do all the killing himself, but was going to make Tony take part out of spite. There was nothing he could do about that, however. He sure as hell didn't want to stir Cross to anger.

Fay brought the skillet over to the table and started spooning potatoes onto the plates before the men. "Oh, come on, Tony," she said caustically, unable to control herself. "Just a little blood and gore on the floor and walls . . . on your hands . . . that's all." Her voice trembled slightly; her hands were slick with sweat. Feeling like a mouse in a cage, she was having trouble containing her hysteria.

"Shut up, teacher," Adler said casually.

"You'll probably hear our screams and wails for the rest of your life, but—"

"I said shut up," Adler said. He chuckled and looked at Tony mockingly. "Why, teach . . . you're gonna have ol' Tony peein' his pants here in a minute."

"You like the blonde's spleen," Cross said to Adler as Fay shoveled potatoes onto his plate. "I like the teacher's." He gazed at her admiringly, his head tilted to one side so he could see her face. He reached up to fold her hair back, but she quickly wheeled toward the stove.

Benji snickered.

"Shut up, you idiot," Cross snapped at him.

Fay could feel the gunman's eyes on her as she returned the potatoes to the stove and picked up the gravy pan. Her hands were shaking so much, she decided to set the pan on the table and let the men dish up for themselves. Benji quickly reached for the spoon.

"Sit back, idiot!" Cross yelled.

Benji froze, his hand on the spoon, face flushing. He glanced at the gunman. "Huh?"

"I said sit back!" Cross looked at Fay, his deeply pitted face splitting with a grin. "The teacher's gonna dish up for us proper."

Fay stood at the corner of the table between Adler and Riemersma, stiffly regarding Cross. She hoped he didn't see her hands or knees trembling; she didn't want to give him that. She wanted to kill him, like she'd never wanted to kill anyone before. And if everything went as planned, she'd do just that. But first she'd have to let him humiliate her.

"Yes," she said, feigning jocularity. "Of course."

She took a leather mitt and picked up the gravy pan, and began spooning gravy on Tony Riemersma's potatoes, then Adler's. Making her way around the table, she dished up for Benji next, and Cross last.

She could feel the man staring at her again, grinning, but she ignored it. When she'd put the spoon back in the pan and had turned back toward the range, Cross suddenly grabbed her skirt and pulled her back with such force that her breath rocketed from her lungs, and she dropped the pan and spoon. They clattered loudly on the floor, and Candace screamed.

A second later, Fay found herself in Cross's lap, straddling his knees backward. He held her with one hand and pawed her vest and shirtwaist with the other, nuzzling her neck. His face was like steel wool scoring her skin, and his breath was hot and fetid with whiskey.

Vaguely she could hear the hoots and catcalls of the other three men. Cross pulled at her shirtwaist until the buttons gave and clattered to the floor. Then, holding her left elbow so hard she thought the bone would break, he tore her corset and pawed her naked breasts. She could feel his tongue—warm and wet—on her neck. The tongue withdrew and he clamped his mouth on her naked shoulder, sinking his teeth into her skin until she saw red and her ears rang.

Instinctively, she twisted around on the man's bony thighs, throwing her right hand up, across her own chest, and digging her nails into his face. "You . . . *fuck*!" she screamed, using a word she'd never used before in her life.

The scratch stunned him momentarily. He released his hold on her arm and in her effort to scramble away from the man, she stumbled and fell headfirst to the floor. The blow dazed her. The ringing in her ears increased, and behind it was the ribald laughter of the men. Behind the laughter, Candace screamed and cried.

"Why, you fuckin' *bitch*!" Cross raged, standing so suddenly that his chair flew back, bounced off a cupboard, and fell on its side.

Fay climbed to her knees, and had just pressed her hands to the floor to push herself to her feet when Cross smacked her, hard, with the back of his hand. It snapped her jaws together and sent her flying backward against a cupboard. Her mouth turned instantly numb and she felt blood on her lip.

"You goddamn bitch! I'll teach you to scratch me!" Cross shouted.

He picked her up and smacked her again. She fell behind Adler's chair, her head numb from the pain, her mouth bloody, her vision swimming. Dimly she was aware of Crystal running into the kitchen against Jody's protestations. One of the men—Fay thought it must have been Adler—grabbed her.

Fay heard a smack and felt the floor shudder. Crystal screamed and Jody yelled.

"No," Fay tried, her cheek pressed to the floor, her head like lead, "Crys . . . Crystal . . . no. . . ." She was thinking of the young woman's baby, knowing it wouldn't take much violence to cause Crystal to lose the unborn child . . . the child for whom she and Jody had waited so long, whom they were so eager to bring into their lives. . . .

"No . . . Crystal . . . hon—"

"Yeah. 'No, Crystal' is right," Cross said through gritted teeth, reaching down, grabbing Fay's hair, and pulling her to her knees. "Nothin' you can do's gonna save the teacher here." He dragged Fay through the kitchen with one hand, grabbing a bottle off the table with the other. Fay grabbed his hand with both of hers, so he wouldn't pull her hair out, and scuttled painfully across the floor on her knees.

He stopped at the door leading to the back of the house. "She's mine for the night. You boys keep a close eye on these others. Don't drink yourselves shit-eyed." Then he opened the door and kicked Fay through the opening like a disobedient dog.

Accepting the violence stoically, keeping her mind on her task, she fell forward and turned. An instant before the door closed, she saw Crystal kneeling on the sitting room floor, Doreen Hawley kneeling beside her. There was blood under Crystal's nose. She was watching, wild-eyed and crying, and Fay caught her eye.

"It's okay," Fay mouthed, trying to give her young friend some hope.

Then Cross grabbed her hair and half-dragged her down the short, dark hall, Fay's knees and hands picking up slivers from the rough puncheon floor, and through another door. He threw her against a dresser, then grabbed her arm and tossed her onto a bed, the cornhusks making a brushing sound beneath her.

"That's it, there we go," Cross said with an air of moronic ebullience.

The room was dark and cold. Enough light penetrated the two windows for Fay to make out Cross's figure. He moved away from the bed and kicked the door closed with such violence the bed shook.

He turned to the bed. The tall black figure, a nightmare apparition or childhood ghost, stood there for several seconds, just staring at her and breathing. He gave a low, laughing grunt, popped the cork on the whiskey bottle, spat it onto the floor, and lifted the bottle to his lips.

Fay waited, numb from the pain of her bruises and abrasions, trying to clear the fog from her brain. As the upraised bottle bubbled and a wet sucking sound filled the room, she felt for the short, serrated knife she'd stuffed into her boot when she'd dropped a potato earlier in the kitchen. It was still there. The slim wood handle felt cool and rough and resolute in her hand.

She'd killed before—a man who'd been about to kill Ben—and the killing had left an acidic, old-penny taste in her mouth for months. It had been a hard thing to do, but with Ben's life on the line, Fay had done it. She'd pulled the trigger. And she'd kill again now. If she didn't, she and all the others wouldn't have a snowball's chance of surviving this hell.

Slowly, trying to be as inconspicuous as possible, she slipped the knife from her boot and brought it up to her side, sliding it just beneath her right buttock. She watched the black figure towering over her.

The drinking stopped, the bottle came down. Cross sighed and belched. He turned, slammed the bottle on the dresser, and sat on the bed. Drunkenly, he brought a knee up and began removing a boot, grunting with the effort.

Now? Fay thought.

No. If she stabbed him in the back he'd cry out and the others would come running.

No, she had to make sure that wherever she stabbed him would kill him instantly, before he could make any noise. Either the heart or the neck. Was the blade of her seven-inch knife long enough to penetrate his heart?

"*Ah* . . . there we gooo!" Cross said as the left boot came free. He tossed it down, struggled out of the other. He stood, unbuckled his cartridge belt, and let it drop to the floor.

"You're gonna like this, teacher. You never had it like you're gonna get it from me." He was unbuckling his pants.

Fay didn't say anything. Her heart beat fiercely. She was shaking with both fear and apprehension, going over and over in her mind what she was about to do.

It had to be fast, which meant she had to have the best possible target, and she had to hit it. If she didn't. . . .

Oh, God. The tension brought tears to her eyes, and she felt on the verge of collapse.

Hold on, Fay, hold on. Think of Ben. Be strong . . .

Cross grunted out of his jeans and kicked them aside. Then Fay lost him in the darkness. Then he was on top of her, grunting and groaning and snarling as he kissed her, running his hard-callused hands across her breasts until her teeth ground from the pain. She kept her left hand on the knife.

"Wait, wait," she whispered. "Let me on top."

He lifted his head to look at her. "Huh?"

"Let me on top."

He stared at her, suspicious. Gradually, a smile pulled at the corners of his dark mouth. He laughed. "All right, teacher, all right. You wanna be on top? Well, that's just peachy with me." He slid off her, rolling onto his back, the bed complaining beneath him.

Carefully, clasping the knife tightly, Fay crawled on top of him, straddling him.

"Hee-hee-hee," Cross howled, grabbing her breasts and kneading them harshly.

"You do like it rough, don't you, teacher?"

"Yeah, I don't mind it a little rough," Fay said.

He pulled her down to him, forcing her lips to his, sticking his tongue in her mouth, jerking it this way and that. Then he withdrew it and bit her lip.

"Uh!" Fay grunted, pulling away. She licked the fresh blood from her lip. The pain was blinding.

"What's the matter, teacher? You said you liked it rough." He laughed.

Fay swallowed and inhaled deeply. "I do, Mr. Cross," she said, leaning down.

She pressed her lips to his. He brought his hands to her head roughly, holding her there as he ground his mouth against hers. As he did, she brought the knife slowly to his throat, turning it in her fist. She held the blade just six inches from his neck. Steeling herself, she brought it back and suddenly forward.

It was like stabbing a feed sack. The blade went in all the way to Fay's fist. Blood flowed hotly over her hand and wrist and onto the bed, squirting and making sucking sounds.

Cross tensed, throwing his head back, dragging a deep breath. Fay lifted her head and slapped her left hand on his mouth, which opened as the man convulsed, trying to scream. He gave several grunts. Fay slapped her bloody right hand on top of the left, scooted up his chest, and leaned with all her weight on the man's opening and closing mouth.

He thrashed at her with his hands, pulling her hair and tearing at her clothes. His legs kicked and he bucked, but his strength was diminished. Fay held on, wincing as she pressed both hands against his mouth, stifling the convulsing grunts, holding his head fast to the blood-soaked pillow.

He stared up at her, eyes wide and darting in furious panic.

Slowly, the convulsing ceased. The death spasms abated to shakes.

Fay loosened her hands on the man's mouth, leaned down, and whispered in his ear. "What's the matter, Mr. Cross? I thought you liked it rough."

The only answer he could manage was a great sigh as his last breath rushed from his lungs.

13

FAY SAT IN the dark room straddling Cross's inert body. She fairly shook from the adrenaline coursing through her veins. Above the blood rushing in her head, she listened for any hint that the others had heard their compatriot's death spasms.

Fay knew there was a pantry between the kitchen and the bedroom she now occupied, so the men's voices were muted. Still, she could hear them speaking intermittently, in a desultory way, as though they'd finished eating and had gone back to their card game and their drinking.

Fay released the breath she hadn't realized she'd held and crawled off Cross's body slowly, trying not to make any noise. She felt as though she'd been clubbed with a heavy branch; she was having trouble getting her thoughts in order.

What now?

She looked around the dark room. Her eyes had adjusted to the darkness, and she could discern more now than just shapes. Cross's gunbelt was one such shape. She bent to retrieve it and stopped. Both her hands were covered in blood.

Shivering both from cold and the grisly substance that had splashed as far up as her elbows, she reached for the bedspread and spent a good five minutes cleaning herself off, keenly attuned to the sounds emanating from the sitting room and kitchen. That done, she straightened and buttoned her clothes, then bent and retrieved Cross's revolver from his holster.

It was a heavy gun, heavier than she was used to, and hefting it in her right hand, she felt a thrill of fear and expectation and power. She'd felt so small and fearful for so long that it was a slightly heady feeling, this feeling of holding a gun instead of being the one at whom the gun was aimed. Her fate was no longer totally in the hands of the outlaws. If they came for her now she had a good chance of shooting one or even two of them.

Hell, if she walked down the hall and opened the door, she might even surprise them enough to get all three. She was thinking this, her heart racing wildly once again, as she hefted the heavy revolver in her hand and pulled back the hammer and raised the gun to her shoulder.

It wouldn't work. The gun was too heavy for her to raise and steady while she aimed. Also, the tension in the hammer was great enough that she didn't think she'd be able to draw it back quickly enough between shots. She might be able to shoot one of them, but while she was struggling with the hammer, the others would have several seconds in which to kill her.

If only Earl's hands were untied, she'd open the door and throw him the gun.

Yes, and get the poor man filled with lead!

Dejected, Fay sat on the bed, holding the gun between her thighs. She had a gun, and one of the outlaws was dead, but she was still in one hell of a pickle. She needed to go for help.

Remembering that the small Durnam ranch sat a mile north of the Hawley farm, just off the trail to Clantick, she stood, walked to a window, and scraped the frost away with her fingernails. It was hard to tell in the dark, but it looked as though the snow had lightened, maybe even stopped falling altogether. The wind was still blowing, however, and blowing the fallen snow in ghostly, diaphanous sheets angling down from the plum-colored sky, where a single star shone dimly in the east.

By all appearances, the storm was on its last legs, and with visibility increasing, Fay had a good chance of reaching the Durnam place—if she didn't freeze. From the chill she felt in the unheated bedroom, and from the furry streaks of frost on the outside walls, she guessed the temperature outside was at least ten, maybe fifteen degrees below zero.

She'd have to dress heavily, and with that thought in mind she looked around the room, where all different shapes and sizes of clothes hung from pegs. When she found what she was looking for, she reluctantly set the revolver on the bed, struggled out of her dress and into two pairs of Earl's long underwear, the smell of rancid sweat not bothering her in the least. The clothes bagged on her, and she had to roll the legs back to practically her knees, but they were warm, and warmth was what she needed.

Walking to the dresser, she rummaged around in Doreen's drawers until she found a couple of pairs of heavy socks, and donned them. Then she pulled on a pair of dungarees that Doreen must have worn while helping Earl in the barn or pigsty—their odor was almost palpable. But again, they fit snugly over the long underwear and would keep the wind out of Fay's bones.

When she'd donned several of Earl's flannel work-shirts and a heavy, moth-eaten wool coat she found under the bed, she looked around for a hat and mittens. Finding neither, she pulled several pairs of socks over her hands, one over her head, and laced up a pair of Doreen's barn boots—knee-high lace-ups and just what the doctor ordered. She tiptoed across the room, pressed her ear to the wall, and listened.

The men were still playing cards. One of them chastised Benji and another whistled through his teeth. Their voices were low drones from far away. Fay could hear nothing from the sitting room, which, she guessed, was good.

"Hold on, just hold on," she whispered as she crept to the door.

She squeezed the knob slowly, soundlessly, and had started to open the door when she remembered the gun. Heading back to the bed, she retrieved it, stuffed it in the waistband under her coat, and went back to the door. The hinges squeaked as she opened it. She stopped, waited a moment, listening, then drew it back with painstaking slowness, wincing against the hinges' quiet chirps, opening it only wide enough to slip through sideways.

In the hall, she pulled the door closed as slowly as she had opened it. She wasn't as careful about holding the knob, however, and when the door came to rest in its frame, the latch snapped home with a crack. It wasn't loud, but it was loud enough to be heard in the other room.

"What was that?" Adler said, looking up suddenly from his cards.

He looked at Tony, who returned the look and shrugged. "The house settlin', I reckon." He'd been drinking heavily, trying to forget about the business in the morning or whenever the storm blew itself out, and the veins in his stubby nose had grown to more than twice their size. He smoked a cigar, and his eyes had a resigned cast as he studied his poker hand.

Adler peered into the sitting room. "What are you folks doin' in there? Earl?"

Earl looked up, wrung out and sleepy and strained to the hilt of human endurance. "What?"

"What are you doin'?"

"I ain't doin' nothin'," Earl growled.

Adler turned his eyes to the blonde, who was kneeling on the floor beside the half-breed, holding a bandage on his shoulder and reclining her head on his chest, her chin in his neck. The half-breed's eyes were closed.

"Hey, Mama," Adler said.

Crystal lifted her head from the half-breed's chest and turned to Adler with a bored, tired look, but her eyes were large and tormented. "What?"

Adler could tell by her look that the sound, a faint crack, hadn't come from her. Doreen and her daughter were on the floor by the stove, their backs to the wood box, half-dozing. They opened their eyes as Adler slid back his chair, stood, walked into the sitting room, and looked around suspiciously, fingering the butt of the revolver hanging low on his thigh.

"Whadja hear, Wayne?" Benji asked.

"Shut up."

Adler turned to the door that led to the back of the house, where the bedrooms were and where, he assumed, there was a stair to the loft or attic. He opened the door quickly, jerking it back. He stood there listening, seeing only the wedge of floor and wall illuminated by the sitting room lamps.

"It was T. J.," Tony said. "You know how much noise he always makes."

Adler knew, and that was what troubled him now. There was no noise.

Turning, he grabbed a lamp off the square center post between the sitting room and kitchen, drew his gun, and walked down the hall to the first door on the left. He listened for a moment, then tapped the barrel of the gun against the door.

"Cross?"

Nothing.

"T. J.?"

He took the lamp in the same hand as his gun, turned the knob, and pushed open the door. He took the lantern in his left hand and lifted it high, scuttling shadows, until a bed was revealed, and on the bed a man.

Adler's heart thumped. He took three quick steps forward, holding up the lamp, the buttery light catching the gleam of T. J. Cross's half-open eyes and reflecting off the thick ruby blood pouring out of his neck.

"Goddamnit!" Adler roared, turning and raking the room quickly with his eyes. Then he was running to the bedroom door and into the hall, turning left, running down the short hall to a back door, pulling up as he lifted the lantern to reveal a slight dusting of snow on the floor.

In the snow was a faint, fresh print.

"Goddamnit!" he raged, jerking the door open and bolting outside.

Fay ran through the deep drifts in the yard, heading north around the pigsty and chicken coop, both of which were nearly completely buried under a wind-feathering drift.

Her heart beat furiously; she felt as though her blood were pure adrenaline. She'd never run so fast, with such abandon, virtually oblivious of the cold air hitting her face like continuous slaps from a hot iron.

Fortunately, the snow was deepest where the wind had

thrown it against the buildings. Away from the buildings and trees and anything else jutting above the ground, it wasn't nearly as deep. In places it was only up to her ankles. Drifts still fingered into the wagon trail she was following along a coulee rim, sometimes several feet high and obliterating the path. But there were enough windblown patches of ground to make the two tracks intermittently discernible in the snowy dark, and keep her heading north where, she hoped, she'd find help.

If she could make it to the Durnam ranch, that is. Adler had to be looking for her by now. Back in the house, she'd hidden in the narrow stairway while he'd gone into the bedroom. Then she'd slipped outside, heading across the yard at a run. Earlier she'd planned to go to the barn and bridle a horse, but that was impossible now.

Only her feet could save her now.

She figured she was at least a minute ahead of the outlaw. She also figured that while he was no doubt a faster runner, she had the advantage because she knew where she was going. All he could do was follow her tracks, which the wind was quickly obliterating behind her.

Also, the enraged Adler had probably run after her as soon as he'd found Cross's body, which meant he wasn't wearing any cold-weather gear. He wouldn't last long out here before having to turn back for a coat and gloves. He could very well saddle a horse and come after her, but that, too, would take time. If she kept running at her current pace, she was sure she could make it to the Durnam ranch by the time he or the other two caught up to her.

Her hope faded, however, when about 150 yards from the house she heard a gunshot. Above the wind it was little more than a muted snap, but she knew it hadn't come from far away.

The gun cracked again, and Fay shot a look over her shoulder. In the blowing darkness about fifty yards behind her she saw a flash, and heard another snap. The sound hadn't died on her ears when she heard a buzz and felt something tear through the left sleeve of her coat. The bullet gave her little more than a nudge, but it threw her off balance in a knee-deep drift. Feet entangling, she fell forward, feeling the sudden icy bite as the snow engulfed her face.

Thrusting her hands beneath her, she pushed herself over, wiped the stinging snow from her eyes, and shot another look down her back trail, where the vague form of a man ran toward her, his boots kicking snow to his knees.

Fay cried out at the horrifying specter of Adler growing out of the darkness before her. She scrambled to her feet and started running, but she knew she couldn't outrun him. After several hard-fought yards through a drift, she decided to make a stand, and dropped to her knees. She quickly removed her right makeshift mitten, stuffed it in a coat pocket, reached under the coat, and removed the revolver.

"You're gonna die, you bitch!" Adler's voice was torn on the wind.

For some reason, it steadied her. This was her last chance, but she felt an inexplicable calm as she turned, bringing the gun up with both hands, extending her arms, pulling back the hammer, and squeezing the trigger at the silhouette growing before her.

The gun roared. The wind slammed the fetid smoke against her face, stinging her eyes. She drew the hammer back again, steadied the gun, and held it there. The figure was no longer closing.

Adler had fallen to his knees in a windswept section of the trail, only about twenty yards before her. He'd lowered his head to his hands, and appeared to waver there in the sweeping gusts of snow, about to fall.

She'd hit him!

Now to finish the bastard off . . .

She tried to steady the gun, but just as she squeezed the trigger, a gust nudged the gun and the shot went wild. Fay wasn't sure if she should walk up to the man and finish him or continue running.

She got her answer when a shadow moved behind Adler. Someone else was coming up behind him.

Without further deliberation, Fay turned and ran down the trail, awkwardly stuffing the revolver back in the coat and donning her sock-mitten, expecting at any moment to hear more gunfire behind her.

But she didn't. Not after she'd run fifty more yards, and not after she'd run another hundred.

After two hundred more yards, she came to a hollow filled with snow, and she had to slow down, trudge through the icy powder as though through a river, holding her hands above her waist. When she came to the other side, she had to rest, her lungs feeling as though they'd been raked with sand, her throat burning, her mouth tasting coppery.

Resting, she gazed behind her, seeing nothing but her own trail through the hollow and the brittle, wind-cleared grass rising on the other side. One star peered through the stormy black sky, like a dim lamp through a dirty window at night.

Not taking any chances, Fay turned and continued along the trail, hugging the ravine, jogging and walking, jogging and walking, trudging through intermittent, drift-filled depressions feeding the coulee on her right.

Twenty minutes later she came to the lip of another

hollow. This was a deeper, wider hollow—practically a coulee itself—filled with snow.

And in the middle of all that snow, as though trying feebly to push out of it, sat a boxlike, two-story cabin, a barn, and corrals. Lights from the cabin's first-story windows made buttery trapezoids on the drifts that all but buried them.

Fay gave a weary sigh and started down.

14

"THERE . . . THAT WASN'T so hard, now was it, Doctor?" Katherine said, as though to a nine-year-old.

The chore of changing the bed linen was finished, and Mrs. Nelson and Little Karla had safely returned to their bed. Katherine pulled the door closed behind her and Evans and flashed the doctor a prim smile.

"Now, your reward for helping this lowly midwife will be supper."

"I'm not hungry," Evans grumbled, turning away from the irritatingly chipper woman and heading for the stairs.

Following him, Katherine said enticingly, "Alice informed me there are several T-bones from a freshly butchered beef in the icebox."

"Enjoy."

"Clyde, really! You're not hungry?"

"Not in the least—only thirsty."

She was about six steps behind him on the stairs. "I tell you what—you go ahead and have your drink—no, have two drinks—and when you're finished, I'll fry you up a succulent T-bone and fill you a heaping plate of potat—"

He'd stopped on the bottom step and turned to her darkly, brown eyes smoldering, the blunt boxer's nose above his heavy red mustache mottling pink with acrimony. "What do you think you're doing?" he said softly, but with a tightness that betrayed his exasperation.

She stopped two steps behind him, mouth still formed around "potatoes," puzzled. "I-I don't understand. . . ."

"It was a fairly simple sentence, Katherine," he snapped. "I'm sure even a woman of your low acumen can process its import."

"Clyde, what in the world is the matter with you? I only offered to cook your supper!"

"No," Evans said, with a quick jerk of his head. "What you're trying to do, either consciously or unconsciously, is make me miserable. Not only did you drag me out in this storm, get me stranded a good five miles from my books and my whiskey, but you're bound and determined to smother me with your . . . your"—he jerked his eyes around, searching for the right words— "your . . . bubbly, petty, insipid . . . *nettling* . . . personality. You have schemed and schemed to keep me from finding even a minimal comfort in my liquor and my Keats!"

She pursed her thin lips and directed a cold look at him, fine lines etched around her eyes. She took a deep breath through her nose. Her voice shook with anger as she spoke slowly, carefully enunciating each word: "You . . . Doctor . . . are . . . an . . . ass."

She pushed past him and headed for the kitchen. "An ass who wants to be left alone!" Evans called after her, feeling some childish need to have the last word.

Cursing under his breath, he wheeled and headed back to his chair, where the green goblet still sat, awaiting his return, only a sip short of the brim. When he'd tossed several stout logs on the hearth, stoking the dying fire to a roar, he sat in the chair, wiggling his way into the leather, getting comfortable. Then he reached for the bottle and replaced the sip he'd taken from the glass earlier . . . the sip he hadn't enjoyed because of Katherine's interruption.

Damn sinful waste of expensive booze.

He corked the bottle, set it on the floor beside the chair, in easy reach, and grabbed his Keats.

"Well, now," he said with a sigh, opening the book in his lap. "There."

He picked up the goblet, holding the blunt stem between his index and middle fingers, steadying the glass with his thumbs. He brought it to his nose and sniffed, the aromatic port instantly conjuring a summery meadow awash with poppies.

He sipped, sloshed the liquor around in his mouth, swallowed, and sighed, a smile growing on his cheeks. He smacked his lips. "Ahhhh."

He set the goblet on the flat arm of the chair and brought the book up to be read, giving another little kick of his legs, adjusting his position for optimum comfort. He focused his eyes on the book and, a pleasant little smile pulling at his mouth and lifting his extravagant red mustache, he went through "Ode to a Grecian Urn," line by line, saying each word in his throat. But by the time he got to the end, softly strumming his vocal chords over ". . . that is all ye know on earth, and all ye need to know," he realized he hadn't understood one word in the whole piece.

Lying between him and the page was the face of Katherine Kemmet. Not her usual scolding, disapproving countenance, but the fleeting look she'd worn a few minutes ago, just before she'd called him an ass. It wasn't her usual expression, and that was why it had stayed with him. It was an undeniable, if faint, look of

honest injury that she'd quickly—too quickly—erased
with her usual scorn, and then stomped away.

He'd injured her, this woman he'd thought to be a
virtual castle wall of obnoxious defenses. And what was
more—this was only a half-formed thought in the doctor's own stoutly mortared consciousness—he'd detected a vulnerability in the woman he'd never known
was there. A girlish innocence, and not an altogether
unattractive one.

These half-formed thoughts came out of nowhere in
the doctor, and were akin to the faint rumblings deep
inside a volcano. If he could have put words to them,
however, he would have said that at the exact moment
when he'd insulted her worse than he ever had, he'd
suddenly felt a bond with the woman . . . indeed, an at-
traction to her. The fact that he'd insulted her when
she'd done nothing but offer to cook him supper made
him feel even more guilty than before.

Morosely he closed the book and sipped the port. It
tasted like turpentine. He continued to sip, however, because he didn't know what else to do with himself. The
fact that he could be in the least bit attracted to Katherine
Kemmet, who had been nothing more than a thorn in
his side for the past seven months, was truly befuddling
and disorienting.

For Evans, who had considered marriage only once
before, and briefly, and who prided himself on getting
full satisfaction from sporting women and liquor, it was
almost like finding out, late in life, that he'd been
adopted. How, in what way, do you continue your life
after something like that?

Well, it couldn't be true, that's all. Probably just the
smell of that goddamn steak she was frying in the
kitchen. The only time he ever wished he had a woman
around—the traditional kind—was when he was hungry.

Most of the prostitutes he'd known couldn't cook.

"Yes, the whores," he said aloud, making a conscious effort to turn his mind in a more comforting direction.

He finished the port in his glass, refilled it, and settled back in his chair to ruminate on all the women he'd had over the years. All the delightful *nymphes du pave* who'd shown him pleasure for a few hours at a time, demanding nothing but a few dollars for their services.

What delightful women, most of them—young and old, ugly and beautiful. There was something so real and honest about a whore. That was what Evans loved. Best of all, they went away when you were done, never requiring the platitudes of wives, never interfering with your private thoughts, your books, and your booze. Never requiring the false civility and empty gentility of marriage—an odious institution founded by ministers and priests to keep people from frolicking as they pleased, as was, by God, only natural.

"To the soiled doves—God love 'em," he said, raising his glass and tipping it back.

But it still did not taste the way it should, and Evans was at a loss to explain why. All he knew was that he felt out of sorts, with no desire whatsoever to read. He was antsy.

It was the damn woman. She was in there eating her steak and the damn smells had made him hungry. After deliberating for several minutes about how he could get her to fry him a steak after he'd insulted her, he refilled his glass, picked up the bottle, struggled out of his chair, and headed for the kitchen.

He stopped in the door. It was a small, well-outfitted kitchen, but not one designed for formal dining. The dining was done in the dining room off the sitting room. Katherine was sitting at a rough wooden table beside the ticking range, cutting a steak smothered in onions. The air was dense with the succulent smell of the meat, onions, and potatoes.

Her face was obscured by the shadows cast by the candle on the table before her, and by the Rochester lamp guttering in a wall bracket over the range. Evans saw her glance up at him quickly, then just as quickly lower her gaze to her plate, where she worked with increasing vigor, cheeks flushing slightly.

Evans was going to make a smart-aleck remark, as he often did out of habit, but seeing her there, eating alone by candle and lantern light, unnerved him, filled him with such a deep, percolating sadness that his throat tightened and a lump swelled in his chest. What the hell was happening to him?

He stood there awkwardly for a full minute, wishing he'd remained in the living room. His initial sardonic impulses having deserted him, he had no idea how to proceed. Finally, he cleared his throat and raised the bottle. "Drink?"

She didn't look at him. "Ha-ha."

"I'm serious," he said, walking into the kitchen. He set the bottle and glass on the table. "Might do you some good."

"It's done wonders for you."

Ignoring her, knowing he deserved that much and more, he looked around for a glass. He could find only a water glass, however, so he filled the goblet and slid it across the table to Katherine, and filled the water glass for himself. He sat down at the other end, having to look around the guttering candle to see her. She said nothing, but continued to eat, cutting her steak vigorously and not giving him so much as a glance.

The candle sputtered and hissed. The storm scuttled around the house like unseen tormentors, occasionally assaulting the timbers with a sudden gust of wind.

Evans sipped from the glass and found himself staring at Katherine. He wasn't sure if it was the candlelight or the shadows or what, but she looked at least ten years younger than usual. But she was only thirty-three, he remembered, surprised.

He'd always considered her at least his age, forty-two. It was the woman's priggish countenance, no doubt, and the severity of the dresses she always wore—the drab grays and dark blues, with lace edging, that didn't so much clothe her body as mask it. And the way her brow was always a little furrowed derisively, mockingly, as though she alone had been sent to judge the sinners and was finding the job both ghastly and amusing.

But when you took a really good look at her, when she wasn't wearing that minister's widow's mask of frigidity and moral arrogance, you could see that she was rather well put together. She was downright pretty, in fact, in an almost classical way, with clean-lined features, smooth, translucent skin, lustrous eyes, and elegant lips. She was a slight woman, too—Evans guessed about five feet four inches tall, maybe 110 pounds.

He sipped again, to cover the slight swelling of his heart. What the hell was this he was suddenly feeling, for God's sake? Lust?

Before, he'd seen her as a menacing ice goddess, the very sight of whom had caused his testicles to withdraw inside his scrotum. Now, suddenly, he was sitting here, half-tight, imagining what she might look like sitting on a bed in only a sheer chemise . . . letting that rich, tawny hair out of the wasp's nest she kept pinned to the back of her head . . . releasing it about her pale, delicate shoulders . . . shoulders that had probably never been kissed by anyone but her late husband, the minister, a man easily old enough to have been her father.

Evans lowered his eyes self-consciously, wondering if

she'd been aware of his stare. He sipped the port again to steel himself, set down the glass, and cleared his throat more loudly than he'd intended. "I, uh . . . I, uh . . . just wanted to say. . . ."

"Yes, Doctor?" she said, suddenly rising and carrying her empty plate over to a dishpan simmering on the range. She dropped the plate in the pan with a splash. "That you're sorry for acting like a fool?" Without looking at him, she turned, walked to a cupboard where another steak sat on a plate, picked up the steak with a fork, and dropped it into a cast-iron skillet on the range.

"Well . . ." he said helplessly, not sure why he felt this compunction, which was completely out of character, to keep apologizing to this woman. He couldn't remember ever having apologized to a woman before in his life, beyond his mother, of course. "Well, I . . . guess so . . . yes."

She absently forked the steak around in the pan, one hand on her hip. He ran a finger around the rim of his glass, confused by his sudden feelings, not sure what to say or how to act. But for some reason he felt compelled to stay here, in this room, and talk to her, this woman he'd spent the past seven months hating. It felt good, in an uncomfortable sort of way, being here with her instead of out there in the living room with only his Keats and his port.

At length it suddenly dawned on him that she was frying another steak, and he looked at her back.

"What are you doing?"

"You have to eat something," she said softly, keeping her back to him.

Her reply inexplicably made the lump in his chest grow. He felt ever so slightly buoyant. The feeling grew keener and keener until emotion flared up within him. "Thank you."

"I guess that's probably my job, isn't it? When the lowly midwife calls the highfalutin doctor out in a storm to deliver a baby, isn't it expected she feed the man?" She said this with not so much her usual bite as amusement.

It hit him then suddenly, like a spear through the skull—she liked him.

For all his crudeness, intoxication, sloth, and droll wit—she liked him.

All her railing before hadn't been because she found him despicably unprofessional. It was because she liked him.

It had been a long time since he'd been liked by the opposite sex. Of course, the Clantick whores all liked him, but only in the way that whores like all their paying customers. Evans had never paid this woman a dime. He had, in fact, done everything he could to insult and avoid her. But here she was, cooking his steak. It was a little off-putting as he sat here and thought about it, but it also gave him a warm sense of belonging.

"How do you like it?" she said.

"Pardon?"

"Your steak—how do you like it done?"

"Oh. Rare."

"Rare it is, Dr. Evans," she said, turning the steak with a sizzle.

The aroma made his mouth water. He felt so warm and fuzzy he decided to have another drink. Very quietly, so she wouldn't hear above the sound of the cooking meat, he uncorked the bottle and topped off his glass. He had no idea what was really happening between him and Katherine; because of the alcohol, his thoughts were sluggish. All he knew was that he was suddenly feeling rather randy and that here was a woman who obviously found him . . . well . . . attractive.

"Go with God, Clyde," he said to himself, and took another swallow of the booze before she forked the steak onto a plate and set the plate before him.

"That sure looks good," he said, enjoying the smell and look of the grass-fed beef but hesitant to eat it, fearing he'd lose his drunk. But what the hell was he going to do, just sit here and stare at it and really make her mad?

He rubbed his hands together eagerly and picked up his fork and knife, but before he could cut into the steak she brought over a pan of fried potatoes.

"Had them warming in the oven," she said.

Good-bye, sweet drunk, good-bye. But he had to admit, the smell and the alcohol had made him feel hollow, so he cut into the steak with a relish not totally feigned.

He ate the succulent meat and greasy, crusty potatoes, all done and seasoned just right, while she washed her own dishes at the pan on the range, and swabbed her end of the table. About halfway through the meal he forgot about the glass of port sitting before him, and found himself thoroughly enjoying the food. He didn't know when was the last time a woman had cooked for him. He usually ate over at Sam Wa's for both breakfast and lunch, and his suppers were usually liquid.

The look on his face must have told the story—that and the eager way he ate, one forkful after another, just like a ranch hand. Katherine said, "Not bad, eh?" with a slight teasing lilt in her voice.

He glanced at her, a little embarrassed by his hunger. "It's . . . it's . . . not bad." He finished the last few bites, washed it down with a sip of the port, and sighed. "Really . . . pretty damn good."

Flushed with self-satisfaction, she took his plate to the washbasin still simmering on the range, and washed it. As she did so, he sat back in his chair and studied her backside, feeling much more kindly toward her in the wake of the meal. He tried to imagine her ass under the long, gray dress she wore, and conjured a nicely rounded pair of buttocks, ripe for the squeezing.

He turned his eyes away just as she turned back to the table, wiping her hands on a towel. "Well," she said, "I guess I better check on Alice and the baby. Then I'll probably turn in, Clyde. Good evening."

"But you haven't finished your drink," Evans complained, gesturing to the goblet. He really did not want to say good night yet; he was enjoying her company.

She smiled good-naturedly, a truly different person than the one he'd come to know. Her voice was gently chiding, in a motherly way. "You know I don't drink, Clyde."

He gave a thoughtful sigh, looking off, then slowly brought his contemplative gaze to hers. "Katherine, I think . . . I think it's time we stopped playing games."

She frowned. "I beg your pardon?"

He got up and walked toward her, staggered slightly, caught himself, straightening, and stopped about a foot away. Even with the food in his stomach, the port had made him light-headed and grand, made him feel, as it often did, that he was the only one who could make sense of the world of human thought and experience. It made him boldly romantic.

He touched her arm. "I know how you feel about me. I know it's taken some time, but I believe I'm beginning to reciprocate."

Her face reddened and she looked down. "I don't think we should talk about this right now."

"I'm sorry it's taken me so long to see things the way you see them. I know how lonely you must be—your husband dead over a year now—and you being a rather"—he smiled at her tenderly—"a rather attractive woman . . . with needs."

She stared at the floor and said nothing.

He took a deep breath, stepped forward, and lifted her chin with his hand. Her head came up, and he pressed his lips to hers. He put his arm around her waist. She was stiff at first, her mouth unwelcoming. But eventually he felt her relax slightly, and her lips parted.

He put his other arm around her, pressing his body against hers as he kissed her. She tensed again, placed a hand on his chest, and gently pushed him away. "No, Clyde, I—"

"I know it's frightening—it's been a long time, but—"

"Clyde, no," she said more forcefully, pushing him away with increased vigor. He didn't let go, however, and she struggled against him. "Clyde!"

"Oh, Katherine, for God sakes!" he snapped, frustrated. "We're not children, and the only man you've probably ever had in your life was the reverend. You're bound to be a little afraid!"

"Clyde!"

"Just give into it!"

"Let . . . me . . . go!" she screamed, suddenly breaking free.

Wheeling, she headed for the door.

"You know you want to, Katherine!"

She stopped suddenly and turned back to him, her eyes filled with tears, face pinched with anguish. "How . . . could you?" she asked thinly.

"How could I what? Give you what you want?"

She just stared at him, shaking her head slightly, totally befuddled. Tears rolled down her cheeks. "You don't have a clue about what I want or need, Clyde Evans. Not a clue. And you know why you don't?"

She paused, as if waiting for him to respond. He just frowned at her, standing in the middle of the kitchen with the shadows shunting across his drink-flushed face, frustrated and befuddled.

"Because you're a drunken fool!" Katherine cried.

She turned and ran from the room. In a few seconds, Evans could hear her feet on the stairs, and her sobs. He stood there, unmoving, for a long time, head reeling.

Slowly he turned, walked back to the table, and sat down, placing his hands on his thighs. Feeling like the brunt of a thousand years of the gods' jibes, he just sat there staring into the kitchen's flickering shadows.

The fire died and the room turned cold.

15

"THAT BITCH! THAT murderin' bitch!"

Adler knelt in the snow, holding his head in his hands and raging. His left temple throbbed where the teacher's bullet had creased him, and he was bleeding like a stuck pig.

"I'm gonna kill you, teacher!" he wailed.

Someone came up behind him and put his hand on his back. "Wayne, what the hell happened?" It was Tony. He was wearing his wool coat, his hat tied down with his scarf. The brim was battered mercilessly by the wind.

"She shot me, that goddamn whore!"

"How bad is it?"

Adler ignored the question. He raised his head and yelled over the wind, "I'm gonna kill you, teacher! Real slooowww!"

Tony grabbed his arm. "Wayne, you're gonna bleed to death if you don't freeze to death first. Come on, we gotta get you back to the cabin."

While Adler climbed to his feet, slipping in the snow, it occurred to Tony—a thought as fast as a lightning bolt—that maybe he should leave the son of a bitch out here. Hell, he could even put a bullet in the raging man's head just to make sure he died. It would be the best thing for Tony and Benji, who'd inherit all the loot, as well as for the people stranded in the Hawley cabin. When the storm let up, Tony and Benji could just take off and give them back their lives, without the killing Wayne and T. J. had insisted was necessary.

But, as always happened to Tony, self-doubt set in, and the thought of him and Benji being on their own soured the notion. Adler was the one who'd gotten them into this, and it would take his cunning to get them out of it.

Tony helped Wayne get turned around in the drift and, one arm on the wounded man's shoulder, guided him back toward the cabin. Wayne shouted, "Goddamn!" at regular intervals, blood pouring over the hand he held to the gash in his temple.

When they got back to the cabin, Tony helped Adler through the back door and down the hall to the living room. Benji was sitting on a chair facing the sitting room, earnestly aiming his revolver at the hostages, like an overgrown kid playing make-believe.

"Where's the teacher?" he asked as Adler and Tony came through the door, covered with snow, faces flushed from the cold.

"Get outta that chair, Benji!" Tony ordered the giant. "Wayne's been hit."

Benji did what he was told, awkwardly moving his big, lumbering frame, knocking the chair over and picking it back up excitedly. When they'd heard Wayne's cries earlier, Tony had ordered him to stay put and keep an eye on the hostages while Tony had gone down the hall to see what was up. He'd come back and reported that T. J. was dead. Then Tony had gone out after

Wayne, leaving Benji again to see after the hostages, and Benji hadn't liked the idea of being left alone with these people. He didn't like having that much responsibility; it shot his nerves.

"What the heck happened, Wayne?" Benji bellowed. "What happened to T. J.?"

Huffing and grunting against the pain of his wound, his face and hand covered with blood, Adler collapsed in the chair. "God*damn* that bitch!" he yelled. "Goddamn her to hell!"

Tony was trying to pry Adler's hand away from the wound so he could get a look at it. Aware that Benji was about to yell out another stupid question, Tony said, "She killed him—that's what happened, you stupid kid. I done told ya that. She killed T. J. Now will you shut up and let me get a look at Wayne's noggin 'fore he bleeds to death?"

Still sitting on the floor by her husband, whose eyes were open now, looking both alarmed and hopeful, Crystal asked Tony, "Did she get away?"

"She mighta gotten away for now," Adler answered her tightly, "but she ain't goin' far. Not in this weather, and not with me comin' after her on a horse!"

"You can't go out there, Wayne. You're bleedin'!" Tony protested.

Adler looked at him. "One of us has to!"

Tony looked wary, not looking forward to the prospect of going out in that wind. "Why?" he said. "She can't get far. Not on foot she can't."

"But what if she can?"

"She *can't!* No woman could. Hell, a man wouldn't make it out there for very long. That wind goes right to the bone!"

"Which way was she headed?" Earl asked him. He'd

been following the conversation with interest, though his hands ached like hell from the tethers.

"North," Adler said.

"There ain't nothin' north," Earl said. "Not for five, six miles, anyways."

"She won't last no six miles, Wayne," Tony said.

"You sure about that?" Wayne asked Earl.

"Yeah, I'm sure."

Adler's eyes jutted to Doreen, who was holding the girl on the floor. "He's lyin', ain't he? There's a place north, ain't there? Not far north."

His kill-crazy eyes wilted the girl, and she sobbed against her mother's shoulder. "Where's Mrs. Stillman, Ma? What happened to Mrs. Stillman?"

"Ain't there?" Adler roared.

The girl screamed as Doreen jumped. "Oh . . . I . . . I wouldn't know if there's a place. . . ."

"Oh, I wouldn't know if there's a place, I wouldn't know if there's a place," Adler sang. "How 'bout if I have Tony ride out and see if there's a place, and if there is a place, I shoot your daughter? Huh? How would that be?"

"Oh!" the woman screamed. "You can't shoot my daughter! You can't shoot my daughter!"

"Well, that's just what I'm agoin' to do if I find out you're lyin' to me!"

"Earl!" Doreen screamed. "Earl, don't let them hurt Candace!" she wailed, clutching the child to her bosom.

Earl looked scared. His eyes slid from his wife and daughter to Adler. He wet his lips, grimaced, and spoke so softly Adler could hardly hear. "There's a place . . . 'bout a mile up. In Frank's Coulee."

"A ranch?"

Earl nodded, his defeated eyes on the floor.

"How many men?"

Earl gave a feeble shrug. "It's a widower with two boys and a daughter."

Adler grimaced and looked down. He was holding a dish towel, which Tony had brought him, to his right temple. His face and chest were covered in blood. "Shit."

"She won't make it, Wayne," Tony said, standing beside him. "I just know she won't."

Adler jerked his head up at the older man, clutching the bloody towel to his head, his left eye squeezed shut against the blood. "You know that for a fact, do ya? Well, none of us thought she'd kill T. J., either, did we?"

"Even if she does make it—what are they gonna do . . . an old man and two hayseed boys?"

"Well, one," Adler said mockingly, "they could come gunning for us. Two, they could maybe hitch a big workhorse to a cutter and go to town for the sheriff." Something dawned on Adler. He got a blank look, then turned sharply to Candace. "Hey, wait a minute! What'd you call her?"

Candace recoiled, sobbing. Her mother stared at the outlaw, slowly shaking her head uncomprehendingly.

"She called the teacher Mrs. Stillman," Adler announced. "I know she did—I heard it."

"So what, Wayne?" Tony asked.

"So Ben Stillman is the sheriff o' Clantick. I know he is 'cause I passed through town a few months back, casing one of the banks. Made it a quick trip, too, when I found out Stillman was there."

"Who's Stillman, Wayne?" Benji asked.

"Used to be a deputy U.S. marshal," Adler said moodily. "Put away my brother about ten years ago. Some whore shot him, put him out of commission for a while. Now he's sheriffin' up in Clantick. That's why I wanted to give that burg a wide berth on our way north." Adler stood and walked to the door, but he was looking at the floor, thoughtfully.

"Goddamn," he said, wheeling, tossing his gaze at Crystal. "She's Stillman's woman, ain't she—our little Miss Beaumont, the teacher?"

Crystal was enjoying his consternation. She almost smiled. "Sure."

Adler stared at her, his upper lip curling angrily.

"Maybe we should just head out now, Wayne?" Tony said mincingly.

"In that?" Wayne said, jerking his head at the window. "You been out there. You know how cold and windy it is, how deep the snow is in places. Hell, we wouldn't make it five miles before our horses played out and we all froze to death."

"We could look for another place to hide out," Tony suggested.

Adler thought about it. Trying to find another cabin to overrun was chancy. They'd gotten lucky, stumbling on a place with folks eager to give strangers the benefit of the doubt. Most folks out here were less hospitable, and good with guns.

"No,". Wayne said, shaking his head. "We stay here till morning. The temperature should lift then." He paused, thinking, holding the ever-reddening towel to his forehead. "But if the teacher gets Stillman on our trail, our asses'll be greased for the pan."

"They will?" Tony said.

"That means we have to go after the teacher, make sure she doesn't get to the ranch up yonder, send someone to town for Stillman."

"We do?"

Adler paused again. A dark light flashed in his eyes. He shook his head. "No."

"Huh?"

"You do." Adler walked over to Tony and put a friendly hand on his shoulder. He grinned devilishly, his silver front tooth catching the lantern light with an evil wink. "I'd bleed to death out there, Tony, my boy."

Before the older man could respond, Adler shoved his face up close to Tony's. *"Go!"*

16

FAY FLOUNDERED IN the deep drifts at the base of the ridge, grunting and moaning.

She'd rolled all the way from the top, her legs having suddenly given out when she'd started the descent. She had no strength after the mile walk through the deep snow and the bone-splitting wind.

When she finally got back on her feet, she looked ahead and saw the lights of the cabin. When she tried to walk toward it, however, her feet wouldn't move. She was chilled, all the way through her muscles to her bones.

She'd never felt this cold. She'd long since stopped feeling anything in her toes but a numb ache, which made it all the harder to negotiate her way through the drifts. She felt as though she had twenty-pound lead balls attached to her ankles.

She finally got her left foot to move, but it caught again in the heavy drift, and she fell forward, on her side. She lifted her head from the snow that stuck its icy hands down her neck and back.

"Help . . . help me," she pleaded, trying to lift her

voice above the wind. It was little more than a chirp. Fay had hardly heard it herself.

Oh, God . . . she'd come this far only to die less than thirty yards from the cabin!

She laid her head back in the snow, hardly feeling the cold anymore. She could feel almost a warmth penetrating her, luring her toward slumber. It would be so easy . . . so, so easy . . . just go to sleep . . .

Then Ben's voice was sharp in her ear. "Woman, you get your ass up and walk! You didn't come this far to go to sleep!"

She gave a start. The voice had been so real.

No, she hadn't come this far to go to sleep. She'd come this far to save Jody and Crystal and the Hawleys. She had a job to do.

Drawing on some hidden strength, she managed to climb to her feet. Slowly, moving one foot in front of the other through the heavy snow that clutched like an undertow, she made her way to the cabin. She practically crawled up the porch steps, and fought her way through the big drift that had been sculpted there by the wind.

She fell forward against the door, in the waist-deep snow. "H-h-help," she cried, softly. "Help . . . help . . . me. . . ."

She pounded feebly with her right hand and stood there, leaning against the door, waiting.

Then she heard something, felt the shudder of movement through the door. It grew louder. The door opened and Fay fell inside, hitting the floor on her face.

"What's this?" Cecil Durnam cried, looking down at the oddly clothed figure at his feet.

He'd been sitting at his kitchen table, reading the Good Book by lantern light and keeping the fires stoked, when he'd heard the noise. Knowing that anyone out in this weather could be up to no good, he'd retrieved his six-shooter from the gunbelt he always kept looped over the peg beside the door, and had meant to pull the door open just a crack. But the weight of this person, whoever he was, had thrown it wide, nearly giving Cecil Durnam a stroke.

His old heart was still doing somersaults, and his knees were fairly quaking, as he gazed at the heap on the floor. It was a woman, he could tell, but one hell of an oddly dressed woman. And he could tell by the paleness of her cheeks she was half froze.

"Heaven forbid," Durnam said.

He stepped over the woman, poked his head out the door, and gazed around cautiously, to see if anyone else was about. Then he returned the old Remington to his pistol belt, squatted down, and lifted the woman in his arms. Her smelly clothes making his nose wrinkle, he kicked the door closed and carried her over to the horsehair sofa, which occupied nearly half of the two-story cabin's tiny sitting room.

He straightened, standing there staring at the woman, fists on his hips, breathing heavily from exertion. She had not been a heavy woman, but Durnam's heart was weak, so weak, in fact, that Durnam was in constant fear of dying and leaving his children orphans. Pneumonia had taken his wife just one year after delivering their daughter, Rose.

The fifty-nine-year-old rancher wasn't thinking of himself at the moment, however. He was trying to figure out who this woman could be—lying there, blinking her eyes groggily, wearing what appeared to be a heavy wool sock on her head, and several more socks on her hands. Her smell was sharp and fetid, but she in no way looked like she smelled. She was lithe under the bulky coat, and had the face of a goddess. A half-frozen goddess.

He was trying to come up with something to say—
Cecil Durnam had always been awkward around
women, which was probably why he hadn't married until he was forty-four—when he heard the door to the loft
stairs creak behind him. He turned to see the pale, fearful
faces of his two sons and daughter staring through the
crack, their blond hair tussled from sleep.

"Pa . . . who is it?" Durnam's eldest, Byron, asked be-
wilderedly. The boy had never wrangled with Indians
but, a devout reader of illustrated newspapers, he knew
their threat was always present. When he'd heard the
door open, he'd been sure it was renegade Blackfeet
come calling, but he'd been too fearful to encourage his
father to be careful.

Durnam gave a helpless gesture and shook his head.
"I don't know. I just opened the door and . . . and here
she is."

The door to the loft stairs opened fully, and the two
boys emerged in their long underwear. The younger of
the two boys, Driscoll, wore a blue flannel shirt. It was
chilly up in the loft, in spite of the two stove chimneys
that went through the second story on their way to the
roof. The girl, Rose, who was nine, followed behind
them, holding to the tail of Driscoll's shirt.

"Mrs. . . . Stillman?" the girl said as she approached
the sofa.

"Huh?" Durnam said.

"Sure enough, it is," Byron said, voice filled with awe.
"Pa, it's our teacher . . . Mrs. Stillman. What's she doin'
out here?"

Fay heard her name as if from far away, and opened
her eyes. She felt drugged; her limbs were hot, and they
ached. Turning her head, she saw the four faces staring
at her, and her reason for being here rolled back into her
consciousness, like the memory of a recent bad dream.

She sat up quickly, but she couldn't move her legs. Rising on her elbows, she focused her eyes on the middle-aged man with thinning gray hair and spectacles, wearing ragged ranch denims and a tattered denim shirt and suspenders.

"You have to help—" Weak from frostbite and because her blood wasn't circulating properly, she lay back and hugged herself, teeth chattering so badly that she could hardly speak. "Go to town . . . get the sher . . . sheriff . . . my hus-husband."

"What's that, miss?" Durnam asked, bending over to get a better look at her. "You're all right now . . . you're safe and sound here at the Cecil Durnam ranch. We'll get the chill out of your bones in no time." He wondered what a fine-looking woman like this was doing out in a raging snowstorm.

Fay shook her head, but before she could speak, Durnam, taking control of the situation, turned to the tallest boy standing beside him. "Byron, go get some more wood, and stoke the stoves to glowing!"

"Right away, Pa!" the boy said, and bolted for the door.

"L-l-listen," Fay pleaded.

Durnam had turned to the other boy, a few inches shorter than the first. "Driscoll, heat some water on the kitchen range and fill the copper tub, but don't get it too hot, just lukewarm. Hear?" He remembered from all his years on the northern plains that lukewarm water was better for frostbite than hot, which could only worsen the damage.

"Right away, Pa!"

"What should I do, Pa, what should I do?" the girl asked, fearful of being left out.

Subconsciously, Fay recognized the girl and both

boys—she taught them all in school—but she was too concerned about the Hawley cabin to think about that now.

"Rose," Durnam said, "you go get your momma's bedclothes out of the trunk. Bring the flannels, hear?"

"I hear, Pa!" the girl said, bolting from the room.

Durnam turned back to Fay. "We'll get you out o' them cold clothes and into a bath in front of the fire, and—"

"Listen to me," Fay said, grabbing the man's arm. She swallowed. Her jaw was so cold it was hard to talk. "The Hawleys are in trouble."

Durnam stared dumbly down at her, wrinkling his bushy gray brows.

With effort, she managed to get her shivering under control. "Someone has to go to town to get my husband . . . Ben Stillman . . . the sheriff."

Durnam's head jerked slightly back. "The sheriff?" His frown deepened. "What are you saying, miss?"

The oldest boy returned with a stack of wood. Both Fay and Durnam ignored him as he deposited the wood in the box by the sitting room stove.

Fay stared straight into Durnam's eyes, summoning all her strength to enunciate the words as forcefully and clearly as she could. "Men came—outlaws—after the storm hit. They'd stolen some money and needed a place to wait out the storm. They attacked us. I got away. They're still there, in the Hawley cabin."

"Outlaws?" Durnam said.

The boy suddenly stopped what he was doing at the wood box, and turned to his father and Fay with concern.

Fay said to Durnam, "Jody and Crystal Harmon are there as well. Jody's been shot. He's . . . he's hurt bad." Fay dug her fingers deeper into the man's arm.

"Please . . . if someone doesn't fetch my husband, they'll all die . . . soon."

Durnam cocked his head and squinted his eyes suspiciously. "Are you sure, miss? It's mighty cold outside. The cold can do funny things to the ole noggin. Why—"

"No!" Fay exclaimed, immeasurably frustrated. "No, no, no!" She swallowed again, sick with urgency and gnawing dread, and shook her head wildly, bringing her other hand onto Durnam's arm for emphasis, pulling herself up. "You have to go to town for Ben! The storm has lightened. It's cold, but you can make it on a horse!"

Durnam continued to stare at her, befuddled and afraid, not quite comprehending what he was hearing. Just a few minutes ago he'd been sitting at his kitchen table reading some Bible verses and listening to the storm pant around his windows. Now this half-frozen woman was telling him the neighbors' cabin was full of outlaws!

He pulled his hand out of Fay's grasp and straightened slowly. He turned to the boy standing by the wood box. Byron's kindled eyes slid between Fay and his father.

Durnam's voice was weighed down with fear and confusion. "She says—"

"I heard," the boy said, bright-eyed with excitement. He'd read about outlaws, but he'd never actually seen one. Now here was his teacher saying there were real, live bandits holed up at the Hawley place. Holy moly!

Durnam turned back to Fay, a grim understanding darkening his gaze. "How many are there?"

"Four. Or . . . three."

"How did you get away?"

Fay shook her head. "There's no time for that. One of them followed me. I shot him—grazed him, I think— but others could be on the way here."

Durnam was thoughtful, fearful, his mind racing.

"Outlaws, you say, huh?" It was a mindless refrain, spoken witlessly while Durnam built his gumption.

Feeling a keen sense of urgency, Fay grabbed the man's arm again, pulling herself to a half-sitting position, and stared coldly into the man's fearful eyes. "Please, Mr. Durnam . . . I'm very sorry to visit this trouble on you and your family, but if someone doesn't head for town now . . . this very minute! . . . innocent people will die."

Durnam nodded, staring, his weak heart straining, making him dizzy. At length, he patted the hand clutched to his forearm. "Okay, miss . . . okay. I'll go to town and get the sheriff."

Fay swallowed with relief and released the man's arm. "Thank you, Mr. Durnam."

Durnam nodded, darkly thoughtful. He turned to his son and sighed. "I think I can make it on old Hector."

The boy shook his head. "I'll go, Pa."

Father and son shared a meaningful look. Durnam knew the boy would have a better chance of making it than he would. For one thing, Byron was lighter, giving Hector an easier time in the snow. For another, the boy had a boy's strong heart, not an old man's sickly one.

The father nodded slowly. Softly, but resolutely, he said, "Get dressed, boy."

17

TONY RIEMERSMA SADDLED his horse in the Hawley barn and wrapped a saddle blanket around his shoulders. He was wearing a cardigan sweater under his coat, and he'd tied a scarf over his Stetson, but the wind was a real bitch, and he figured he'd need every bit of extra warmth he could carry.

He didn't know why in hell Adler couldn't have sent Benji, who was a good twenty years younger than Tony. The big idiot had plenty of extra fat to protect against the cold, and he'd never had any of the qualms about killing that Tony did. By rights, Benji should be out here freezing his oysters, not Tony. But Tony wasn't going to argue with Wayne. He always knew when to argue with that madman, and he'd been able to tell by the look in Wayne's eyes that tonight was not the time.

Adler had sent him out here out of meanness, pure and simple.

"The stinkin' son of a nasty God-blame bitch is gonna be old someday hisself," Tony grumbled as he led his horse through the open barn doors, ducking his head as the wind hit him so hard he almost stumbled backward.

The horse jerked its head up and pulled at the reins, reluctant to leave the relative warmth of its stall. Its eyes were wild, rolling back in its head. Seeing them, Tony gave a shudder. When a horse was afraid of the weather, it was time for its rider to be afraid, too.

When he'd fought the doors closed, Tony climbed into the leather. He had to spur the horse and jerk and whip the reins to get him headed north, away from the barn, the horse whinnying and giving a couple of half-hearted bucks. Finally, the horse relented and Riemersma pulled him onto the trail that hugged the coulee, following the tracks left by the teacher, most of which were the faintest indentations in the drifts. Only the deepest tracks in the low-lying drifts remained.

Huddled down in his coat, holding his collar closed at his neck with one hand while steering the horse with the other, Riemersma guessed the temperature must have been at least twenty below zero, sinking probably twenty degrees lower than that with every wind gust, which pelted him with stinging, slanting snow. Each blast brought the line-back dun up short, and Riemersma had to gouge the horse with his spurs to keep it moving.

The sky was black. Between waves of blowing snow, stars kindled. Riding along, fighting the damn horse every step of the way, Tony Riemersma felt as though he'd been exiled to oblivion. And that was exactly what Adler would to do to him, too, if he let the teacher warn the neighboring cabin. Exile him to oblivion with a bullet between his eyes.

The mile ride took what seemed like forever, with Tony having to get off and pull the horse through several of the deeper drifts, cursing the skittish mount by note and rhyme, knowing that if the goddamn teacher made it to the other cabin, he was done for. If Adler didn't get him, some gun-handy cowpoke from the neighboring ranch probably would.

All Tony wanted was his share of the loot and a long, happy retirement in Mexico. He figured he'd cracked between thirty and forty bank safes from Tacoma to Santa Fe, when he wasn't pulling random, petty robberies here and there about the West, and by God he deserved a rest . . . outside of a jail, that is. Just some dark-eyed señoritas, a few bottles of good tequila, Cuban cigars, and a balconied hotel room overlooking the ocean . . .

When Tony came to the coulee in which the Durnam ranch sat, he was thoroughly exhausted. He felt panicky, as well, because he hadn't caught up to the teacher, whose tracks led down the ravine, erased as he watched by the glittering snakes of drifting snow.

"Goddamnit all to hell, teacher, you're gonna get me fried."

He dismounted and knelt down beside the agitated horse, raking his eyes over the cabin sitting in what looked like one gigantic snowdrift, its first-story windows nearly buried. There was a barn and a few other outbuildings, but they were dark. No bunkhouse, it appeared. That was good. Tony hoped this was just a small, ten-cow outfit, with no gun-savvy cowpokes. Because it appeared he was going to have to kill everyone in the cabin, to make sure no one sprang for town.

He grunted and gave his head a worried shake. Could he do that?

Well, by God, he had to. It was them or him. And he had, sure as horns on a stud elk, worked hard and long to retire in old Mexico, not molder away in the territorial prison down in Deer Lodge until they hanged him. Or, worse yet, die out here in this chilblain storm. He was going to see the ocean before he died.

Thinking of the Gulf, which he'd seen only in pictures—a failing that the cold he felt leaking into every corner of his body made him even more bound and determined to rectify—he got back on the horse and encouraged the animal down the hill. He pulled up behind the stable that sat about fifty yards from the house, and dismounted. Tying the animal to a corral post, he shucked his Winchester and crept to a corner of the stable, poking a look around the corner.

Before him sat the house. Now most of the windows were lit, even a few upstairs. He could tell that the teacher was inside, all right, and had warned the inhabitants. The downstairs windows showed people scurrying this way and that, carrying what looked like articles of clothing—sweaters, scarves, mittens, and coats.

A couple of the people appeared to be children. Another was a man about Tony's age, with thinning gray hair and a sparrow chest and thick glasses. He moved the slowest but he was talking a good deal. He was too far away to tell for sure, but Tony thought he looked befuddled and anxious.

Yeah . . . the teacher had made it, all right, and told her story.

But Tony took comfort in knowing there weren't any young cowpokes about—men like Adler. No matter what Adler thought of Tony's abilities, Tony was sure he could take the old man out of action, as well as the teacher, especially after what she'd done to T. J. Cross. It was a matter now of letting people live and getting caught, or killing and running free . . . all the way to the Gulf of Mexico.

The children would be more difficult. He might have to kill the oldest one, who appeared fifteen or sixteen. The others he could tie up good and tight. They probably wouldn't be found before Tony, Adler, and the big idiot were well on their way to Canada.

Tony jacked a shell in the breech of his Winchester, and was about to start toward the house when the cabin door opened. He jerked back behind the stable and peeked around the corner, his rifle held at the ready.

There were voices, a boy's and a man's, but the wind covered their words. The boy and the man, bundled against the cold and holding rifles in their hands, stepped outside. Holding a lantern up high, the old man peered around suspiciously, his head turning toward the stable. Tony jerked his head back and waited.

More voices, just barely audible. Then the door closed with a wooden click.

Carefully, Tony peered around the stable. The old man and the boy were walking this way, toward the stable!

Tony's heart did a flip. He stiffened, mind racing. If he shot them both right now—two easy shots at this distance, as easy as the soldiers had been—he could head over to the cabin and kill the teacher. Then all he'd have to do was subdue the other kids, and he'd be on his way to Mexico.

Before he could learn whether or not he had the gumption to do it, another plan occurred to him. Why not wait until these two had ridden away from the stables, then follow them and kill them a good distance away from the ranch? Far enough away that no one in the cabin would hear. That way he wouldn't have to kill the teacher, only these two. The teacher and the kids left in the cabin would think the old man and the boy had safely ridden off to get the sheriff.

Only, the sheriff wouldn't come, because no one had summoned him . . . and Tony would ride back to Adler with his head up, having successfully completed his mission.

Satisfied with the plan, Tony stiffened against the stable wall, trying to make as little noise as possible. He heard the doors open, and then he saw the light through the loose chinking between the logs. If he could see their lantern light, the boy and the old man could see his silhouette, so he crouched down, making himself as small as possible. Then he noticed his horse, standing there with its head down, looking none too pleased with the situation. All the animal had to do was nicker or blow one time, and Tony's presence would be exposed.

Shit.

Crouching, Tony trudged through the knee-deep snow and placed both mittened hands over the horse's nose, holding the animal's head down. As he did so, he watched the lantern light waver through the cracks in the stable walls.

The old man and the boy were obviously saddling horses for the ride to town. They must have been nervous, because they weren't saying much. The old man gave a few clipped orders, but that was all. Tony wished they'd hurry. He could tell by the resistance in the lineback's snout that the horse was feeling more and more insulted, and angry.

Finally the lamp dimmed and Tony saw the shadows in the stable fade. He heard the door open. Then the stable was dark. The old man and the boy had apparently led their horses outside.

Tony released the line-back and edged back to the corner of the stable, stepping away from the building until he could see the old man and the boy. Just outside the stable doors, the boy was mounting a stout, broad-backed horse that had to stand at least seventeen hands high. The old man just stood there holding the lantern, his own rifle, and the boy's. He had no horse.

What the hell did that mean? The old man wasn't going? He was just seeing the boy off?

Retreating to the darkness behind the stable, Tony ran his tongue over his teeth, pondering the situation. He was so cold that even his eyeballs ached, but his heart grew light. If the boy was heading for town alone, Tony's job would be all the easier. He'd just catch up to the lad a few hundred yards from the cabin—out of hearing range, which wouldn't be far in this wind—and shoot him in the back. Then he'd ride back to the Hawley cabin and warm himself at the stove, partake of a few more shots of Wayne's whiskey.

In the morning they'd all leave for Canada . . . with the loot they'd now be splitting three ways instead of four! True, Adler would probably still insist the other hostages die, but Tony figured he could do it now. He'd stay drunk, put his gun to their heads, and close his eyes. Small price to pay for a window overlooking the Gulf of *Méjico*.

He waited behind the stable, peeking around the corner, until the boy had ridden off on the big, shaggy horse, and the old man had gone back inside the cabin. Then Tony snugged his rifle back in the saddle boot, took up the line-back's reins, mounted, and coaxed the horse through the dunelike drifts directly behind the stable, keeping well away from the house's windows until he was at least a hundred yards from the property.

Then he drew the horse up short and turned him in the direction the boy had taken.

"Okay, here we go, night's about over," he said aloud, kicking savagely at the reluctant line-back's flanks.

The boy had taken what appeared to be a horse trail up the other side of the coulee, through a cut in the high bank. Alhough the big horse's tracks were filling

quickly, Tony could make them out well enough to follow them, urging his own horse with raspy curses and
whipping his reins at the animal's neck.

At first he rode just fast enough to keep pace with the
boy. But when he figured he'd gone about three hundred
yards from the ranch, and was riding out across a table
where the unimpeded wind lashed brutally at his face,
nearly blowing the line-back over at times, he goaded
the horse even more savagely with his spurs.

"Come on, you old nag, come on!" he whispered
hoarsely in the animal's twitching ears.

From the hoofprints in the snow ahead, he could tell
the boy was measuring his pace, not wanting to use up
too much of the big horse's strength at once. After all,
they had a five-mile trip through a savage wind and intermittent three- and four-foot drifts.

Tony thought he was probably gaining on them,
slowly but surely. It wouldn't be long now. Another five
minutes and he'd see them. He hoped the kid wasn't
looking behind him, but even if he was, he wouldn't see
Tony much before Tony could shoot him.

The line-back cantered, snorting angrily and shaking
its head. It was a cussedly stubborn beast, and Tony
regretted buying the animal from a farmer down by
White Sulphur Springs, but it was doing its job, by God.
The boy's prints were getting cleaner and cleaner, which
meant he and the big horse couldn't be much more than
thirty, forty yards ahead, and the gap was narrowing
with every reluctant beat of the line-back's awkward
gait.

Tony's heart thumped excitedly. He squeezed his eyes
closed, warming them, then opened them and reached
for his rifle. He pulled the hammer back and brought the
gun up before him, ready to shoot as soon as he saw the
horse. He didn't want to see much of the boy, just

enough of his back for a clean shot. He sure as hell didn't want to see his face. Seeing his face would only trouble Tony's dreams later, when he was trying to enjoy the señoritas and the ocean.

About ten more paces, and the broad ass of the big horse formed in the darkness ahead, the back hooves kicking up gouts of snow, which the wind tore away like desert sand. Tony raised the rifle and waited for the boy to form in the darkness, as well.

But all that formed was the horse's empty saddle.

The boy wasn't there!

Tony's eyes squinted and his cheeks wrinkled with exasperation. Then his heart leaped. He'd been duped!

But the realization had hardly had time to form when Tony heard a muffled snap and felt something warm and fast plow into his chest, nearly unseating him. It took his breath. He froze, a great dolor overcoming him, and he rolled lazily out of the saddle, his right boot catching in his stirrup and dragging him for several yards before it came loose. He came to rest on his back, boots facing the direction he'd been heading.

Oh, God, oh, God . . . what the hell . . . ?

Tony felt something heavy and wet on his chest. Then he felt nothing but a generalized numbness. His ears rang. Above the ringing he heard footsteps in the snow, the feet of someone running. As the feet approached he heard the heavy breaths of the runner.

Then the boy was standing over him, staring down at his face. He cradled a rifle in his arms, like a hunter. He was breathing heavily and staring down at Tony, awestruck.

"I got you, didn't I?" the boy said excitedly.

Tony swallowed, suddenly realizing that the kid had shot him.

"Yes," he said softly.

Puzzledly, almost angrily, the kid said, "Didn't ya know I'd scout my back trail, to see who and how many were trailin' me? Heck, in every magazine story, the good guys always scout their back trail!"

Tony had no response to that. The world was dimming, becoming a very peaceful dream in which there was no wind or snow or stubborn horses. He stared up at the boy and cracked a smile. The boy shook his head, turned, stuck two fingers in his mouth, and whistled loudly. Then he trotted off, mounted the big horse, who'd returned for him, and cantered off in the stormy night.

Tony died, but not before the line-back dun had turned around and galloped back toward shelter.

18

CRYSTAL TORE ANOTHER strip of cloth from the hem of her dress, balled it in her fist, and held it to Jody's wound. At the rate she was tearing strips from her dress, she'd soon be in little more than pantaloons and bloomers. But she'd finally gotten the blood stopped. Well, if not stopped, at least slowed to a trickle. There was still the problem of the bullet, however. It needed to come out, and it needed to come out soon.

She gazed down into her young husband's face. Jody's eyes were closed; he was sleeping. His skin was pale, though, and Crystal didn't like that at all. It was the blanched, waxy color of dead people.

The thought of Jody dying sent a shudder through Crystal's entire body. She'd known Jody since they were both eight years old, for both their families had ranched in the Two Bears, and she knew him better than anyone, including herself. She loved him more than life itself. They'd been so eager to start a family that when Doc Evans told her she was pregnant, they danced a jig around their cabin and fell into an afternoon of blissful lovemaking and lazy, hopeful talk of the future.

She would deliver soon, in about a month or so, and if anything happened and Jody couldn't be there . . . Well, if Jody died, Crystal hoped these madmen killed her, too, because she didn't want to go on living without him . . . didn't want to bring their child into the world if Jody wouldn't be here to help her raise it.

Tears rolled down her cheeks. "Jody, please don't die," she begged him through a whisper.

"I ain't gonna die, Crystal Johnson," he said to her surprise, his eyes closed. "Stop thinkin' so negative."

He opened his eyes and gazed back at her, a thin smile drawing the corners of his mouth up slightly. She returned the smile, smoothing his hair back from his forehead. "How you feelin', possum-player?"

"I been better, but not too bad. A little chilly. I'm gonna make it, though. Don't you worry now."

She glanced at the kitchen, where Adler and Benji sat at the table, then turned back to Jody. "Oh, Jody, how are we ever going to get out of this?" Her voice cracked; she'd never felt so panicked, so terrified and hopeless.

Jody took her hand in his. "We just have to hope Fay made it over to Cecil's. Cecil'll send one of his boys to town. Probably ol' Byron. That kid reads a lot, but he's got sand. I trailed with him on roundup."

"But what if she doesn't make it? It's awful cold out there, and she's on foot."

Jody squeezed her hand and gazed at her directly. "She'll make it."

"Wayne sent the older one after her."

Jody faked a smile again. "Fay'll have him bowin' and bendin' like a pig over a nut." He shook his head with genuine amusement. "I can't believe she killed Cross. That woman is somethin' else."

"Yeah, she's somethin' else, all right." It was Adler, sitting alone at the far end of the kitchen table playing solitaire. Benji had gone out behind the cabin for more wood. "She's somethin' dead by now."

He hooted, but it wasn't genuine. He was uneasy, which was why he kept drinking and smoking, tossing down cards, then getting up to pace the cabin. A few minutes ago he'd kicked Earl over in his chair. When he'd gone back into the kitchen, Crystal and Doreen had gotten Earl upright again, ignoring Adler's laughter at their struggle. Poor Candace had cried harder, with more sheer horror than Crystal had ever heard before. Now the girl was sitting again in her mother's lap, face swollen from her tears, eyes staring unseeing out the window.

Crystal turned to Adler sharply. "If she makes it—and I'm betting she will, because I know her—and if someone gets to town for her husband, you won't have a chance in hell. He'll kill all of you."

"That right?" Adler said, turning his bright, drunk gaze on her.

"If I was you," Crystal added, ignoring Jody's admonishing grip on her hand, her anger and desperation getting away from her, "I'd hightail it right now."

"You would, would you? Well, I'll tell you this, Mama—I ain't goin' nowheres till daylight. I'd rather face Stillman than this storm. So you can just forget about that right now. You don't want me leavin', anyway, 'cause when I do, I'm gonna leave a whole cabin full o' dead folks." He inhaled deeply on his cigarette and grinned as he blew the smoke toward her.

"I don't think you'll kill us," Crystal told him, knowing she was pushing her luck, but feeling too desperate and rattled to shut up. "I don't think you have it in you. Your dead friend in the other room had it in him, but I don't think you have it in you to kill a pregnant woman, a mother, a child, and two husbands."

Adler laughed, throwing a card down with a drunken

flourish. "You don't think so, do you, Mama? I guess you're just taken by my pretty face, but I'll tell you this—I killed before. And I don't mean just once or twice, neither. And the only reason I haven't killed you and your half-breed man there and the others is because I just didn't feel like stinkin' the place up with your blood." Now he was staring at her darkly from across the cabin, his evil almost palpable. "And now it turns out I might be takin' one o' you with me."

"*With* you? Why?"

Adler's cold smile returned. "If ol' Stillman knows we got us a pretty young woman in the family way along for the ride—or a little girl—and if he knows we'll kill them if he follows us, he might decide it's best if he lets us go."

Crystal narrowed her eyes at the man. "You're a real man, Wayne. You do your parents proud."

"I don't think so," the outlaw said smugly. "I kilt my ma." He spread a silver-toothed smile and gave a wink. "Took a hatchet to her and my uncle when I caught 'em ruttin' in the smokehouse." He snickered deep in his chest. "What an awful mess that was!"

Just then Benji came in the hall door with a load of split pine. He walked over to the wood box and dumped the load. He crouched down to retrieve several pieces for the stove. As he did so, the walnut butt of his revolver hung only about six feet from Crystal, who stared at it self-consciously, sliding her gaze between it and Adler, who'd gone back to his solitaire in the kitchen, a satisfied smirk on his face.

Impulsively, heart racing, ears ringing, Crystal reached for the smooth wooden butt of the gun hanging only a few feet away. But before she could get her arm stretched, Jody grabbed it down.

Crystal shot him an angry glance. Jody gave his head a slow, feeble shake, and closed his eyes.

"You might thank him, Mama," Adler said, looking over his cards.

"What's that?" Crystal said.

"Your husband just saved your life."

Byron Durnam knew he shouldn't do it, but after slogging through the snow of a deep swale, he climbed off old Hector to give the horse a blow. Hec was one hell of a horse, as his dad always said, but this wind and these drifts had tired him. The Percheron's breath was raspy, and he'd coughed and shook his head several times. Byron could tell by the way the horse's flesh quivered beneath his shaggy coat that the cold was getting to him, too.

Byron knew he didn't have time to waste—Mrs. Stillman had made it pretty clear that the bad men in the Hawley cabin could start killing anytime—but he didn't see how giving Hector a two-minute breather could make much of a difference. It wouldn't do anyone any good if ol' Hec went down in a drift with a stroke, as Byron knew could happen to a horse old Hec's age.

"Sorry, big fella, but it's time to move," he said, climbing back into the saddle, which he thought Hector tolerated well in spite of his being mostly a dray and plow horse, rarely the riding kind.

The wind pummeling him and Hector like a thousand icy fists, he rode on, keeping his head down, out of the brunt of the blast, squinting his cold-aching eyes at the trail. Hector seemed to know the town road by heart. Several times Byron thought they'd lost it under the snow; then a familiar landmark appeared, or a snow-swept stretch of road, reassuring him the big horse knew exactly where he was going.

The boy had never been so happy to finally see the shanties and cabins outlying Clantick—dark, shabby structures crouched against the wind and ravaged by the snow, which clung to their walls like white moss. With the virgin snowbanks covering the streets, not a soul in sight, and all the storm-buffeted houses looking abandoned, like boats on a strange, white sea, it was only the wood smoke wafting on the wind that reassured Byron he wasn't the only one left alive.

Slogging through the drifted streets, he stopped at the Stillmans' white frame house on French Street. Pounding on the door and peering in the window, finding no one home, he got back on Hector and made his way over to the jailhouse on First. His heart lightened when he saw the buttery glow of a lantern behind the gold-leaf letters on the window reading HILL COUNTY SHERIFF.

His extremities chilled to the point that he couldn't feel them any longer, he as much fell as climbed out of the saddle. Not bothering to loop Hector's reins over the hitching post—the horse wasn't going anywhere in this weather—he kicked through the snow under the awning and pounded on the door with one deerskin-clad fist.

"Sheriff Stillman," he called.

There was no reply except for the wind funneling under the wood awning and battering the boy senseless, keeping his cheeks aflame with frostbite.

"Sheriff!" he called. At the same time, he punched the latch. The door fell in, bringing Byron with it, plunging into the arms of Sheriff Stillman.

"Whoa there!" Stillman said, as he clutched the boy in his arms, trying to keep the lad on his feet. Having told Leon to go on home, the sheriff had been dozing in his chair when he'd heard the pounding on the door. Immediately thinking of Fay, he'd come running.

"Steady, boy, steady!" Stillman said. "What in the hell are you doing out in this weather?"

The boy looked up at him, face crimson in places, white in others, frostbitten. The eyes were urgent. "There's trouble, Sheriff . . . out at the Hawley place!"

"Trouble?" Stillman said, feeling a minnow of apprehension flutter in his gut.

"Yessir. Your wife sent me."

Stillman's heart drummed. "Fay?"

The boy swallowed with effort—the cold had constricted his throat—and nodded. When he spoke, it was with forced calm, an air of tethered nerves. "There's bad men in the cabin. Mrs. Stillman, she got away, but Jody and Crystal and the Hawleys . . . they're still inside!"

Stillman just stared at the boy, his mind racing. The door stood open behind them, fluttering the lanterns, but Stillman made no move to close it. All he'd comprehended so far was that Fay was alive. When the rest had sunk in, he frowned skeptically. "Bad men?"

The boy nodded. "That's what your wife said. They're in the Hawley cabin, and Jody's been shot."

"Where's Fay?"

"Our-our place," Byron said, trying to keep his teeth from chattering.

"You're a Durnam lad, aren't you?"

"I'm Byron, sir."

Deep in thought, Stillman moved to the door and closed it. Gravely, he turned back to the boy. "Who are they and what do they want?"

"Mrs. Stillman just said they were outlaws . . . with a saddlebag full o' greenbacks. They got caught in the storm after a holdup and needed a place to stay."

"How many?"

"There's only two left, sir." The boy nearly smiled.

Stillman looked at him with surprise. "What happened?"

"Mrs. Stillman got one, and"—Stillman could tell the lad was trying hard to look humble—"and I got another as he trailed me out from the ranch."

Stillman allowed himself a lopsided grin. "Nice shooting, kid."

"Thank you, sir."

Stillman rubbed his jaw. "Jody's been shot, you say? How bad?"

Byron told him what Fay had said, that Jody had been hit in the shoulder and he'd lost a lot of blood, but that he was conscious off and on.

"Crystal and the others?" Stillman thought of the unborn baby.

Byron shrugged. "Mrs. Stillman said just Jody's been shot, but she was worried, Mr. Stillman. You gotta know, she was worried. They said they're gonna kill everybody in the cabin in the morning."

"In the morning, eh?" Stillman's mind wheeled this way and that. The snow, the wind, the distance from here to the Hawley cabin. Fay was all right, but . . . Jody, Crystal, their unborn child, and the Hawleys . . . they could all die.

How in the hell could Stillman get to them in time to save them?

Well, first things first.

"Boy," he said. "You stay here and mind the store, will you? Keep the fires stoked? I have three prisoners back there, but you're not to go near them, understand?"

In spite of the chill that had penetrated his core, the boy's ears pricked up. After all the night's excitement, now he was going to tend a jailhouse! He did his best to look casual, all in a day's work. "Yes, sir. Can I tend my horse, sir?"

"Sure, you can. Stable him out back with mine. Just make sure the stoves stay fired. Help yourself to hot coffee and any vittles you can find."

"You goin' out there?" Byron asked.

Stillman already had his Henry down from the wall rack and was checking the loads. "One way or another."

19

STILLMAN HEADED EAST up First Street to Mrs. Lee's, the whorehouse where Leon McMannigle kept a room for free, his only payment being his presence, which drastically reduced the amount of trouble normally found in most houses of ill repute. Stillman's countenance was grim as he waded the deep drifts lining the boardwalks, dressed in his buckskin mackinaw, wool scarf, and fur hat with earflaps, clutching his Henry rifle in his right mitten.

He was thinking of Jody and Crystal Harmon and the Hawleys. He was thinking of Fay, silently chastising himself for not riding out earlier to find her. If he had, he might have been able to foil the renegades' game. He knew his chances of making it, with the storm thickening, had not been good, but he still couldn't help feeling like a fool for sitting around playing cards with Leon while all hell broke loose out at the Hawleys'.

He pounded on the door to Mrs. Lee's for a full five minutes before he heard the inner stairs creak and befuddled female voices rise. The bolt was thrown and the door opened. Leon appeared with two rumpled girls behind him, all looking bleary-eyed. The deputy was wearing a black velvet robe with hand-stitched designs—a gift from one of the girls, no doubt. Blinking his sleepy eyes, he held his six-shooter aimed at Stillman's waist.

"Ben?"

"Sorry to wake you, but we got trouble, hoss."

Stillman informed Leon of the situation while the black man dressed in his small, cozy room upstairs. The sheets and quilts were rumpled, and both pillows were dented, which meant a girl had been here before Stillman had come. There was the vague smell of perfume mixed with the smell of the coal stove, glowing in a corner.

Leon shook his head darkly and sat on the bed to pull his boots on. "So what's the plan?"

Standing before the door, his fur hat in his hands, his face flushed with concern, Stillman shrugged. "We ride out as far as the Durnam ranch, thaw out, switch horses, and continue on to the Hawleys'. I guess we won't know what we're going to do there until we have to do it."

"How bad's Jody hurt?"

"Shoulder," Stillman said, taking a deep breath and glancing restlessly around the room. "He's lost a lot of blood. That boy's like a son to me; if they've killed him . . ." He let the sentence go, grinding his teeth together.

"He'll make it; he's tough," Leon said. Grabbing his hat and pulling on his coat, he headed for the door, and Stillman followed him out.

They were on the trail—if you could call the vaguely delineated crease in the snow outside Clantick a trail—a quarter hour later, cantering their horses over open patches, walking them when the snow climbed to their hocks. It was so cold that both men lost the feeling in their fingers and toes—in spite of wool-lined mittens and boots—only a short way from town. Their mustaches and eyelashes iced. Their cheeks burned. The wind was so swift it nearly blew them from their saddles. Occasionally, the horses stopped and needed coaxing to continue. Several times the riders had to dismount and lead the animals through the four-, five-, and six-foot drifts.

Stillman figured they'd reached the halfway point around four a.m. They and the horses were half-frozen and exhausted, but they did not take time to rest. The urge to make the Hawley cabin before any of the hostages were killed, before Jody Harmon died from his wound, was burning deep within both men.

Stillman was too cold to feel relief when, an interminable hour later, he saw the lights of the Durnam house, intermittently dimmed by blowing snow.

"I'll take the horses to the barn," Leon said as they rode into the yard.

"You're as cold as I am," Stillman retorted.

The frosty-faced deputy reached over and grabbed the reins out of Stillman's hand. "Get over to the house and see your wife, goddamnit!"

Stillman looked at his deputy, whose eyes were determined. Stillman would have smiled if the muscles in his face hadn't been frozen; instead, he merely shook his head and dismounted. While Leon headed for the barn, Stillman trudged stiffly through the snow to the cabin on feet that felt like cinder blocks.

Durnam answered his knock on the door holding a pistol in his hand. "Well, I'll be goddamned," the rancher exclaimed in an awe-filled bass. "My boy made it to town!"

"He made it," Stillman said, looking around past Durnam.

Fay sat in a chair by the fire, clad in a buffalo robe, her bare feet soaking in a pan of water. A blond girl in a flannel nightie sat worshipfully at Fay's feet. Fay held a stone mug in both hands. Her eyes found Stillman's, growing wide with eager surprise. In a second, she'd set the mug on the small table beside her and was out of the chair in a bound, splashing water as she ran across the kitchen.

"Ben!" she cried, throwing her head against his chest, her arms around his neck. "Thank God you made it!" Her rich, dark hair was loose and flowing about her shoulders.

"Yep . . . I made it," Stillman said, holding her tightly, suddenly no longer feeling the cold. He ran a mittened hand through her hair. "Thank God . . . thank God you're safe."

"I'm the only one," she said, lifting her head to look into his eyes. "I got away, but the others . . ."

"I know, they're still in trouble. Not for much longer, honey. I promise you that."

Her eyes took him in then, seeing the pale patches in his otherwise flushed cheeks, his frosty eyebrows, lashes, and mustache. "Oh, God, Ben . . . you're half-froze! Come in here . . . sit down." She took his hand and led him to the chair she'd been occupying by the fire. He sat down with a grunt, feeling his bones creak as he moved.

"You have to get out of those clothes," she said.

Stillman shook his head. "There's no time for that. We'll just sit by the fire for a few minutes and thaw out. Then we have to get over there."

"We?" Durnam asked. He stood before the door, holding the revolver down at his thigh. His daughter sat before the stove, eyes riveted on Stillman, the man who'd come to save the poor people at the Hawley farm.

Stillman made a feeble attempt to remove his right mitten. Fay helped him. He said to Durnam, "My deputy's with me. He's putting our horses in the barn.

They're nearly froze. We'll need to borrow a couple of yours." His jaw was so cold he had to spit the words out like prune pits.

"Snotty and Tom can handle it, Pa!" Stillman turned to see a boy, a smaller version of young Byron and with slightly darker hair, standing between the kitchen and living room.

"Bundle up and get 'em saddled good and tight, Driscoll!" Durnam ordered.

The boy wheeled to the clothes pegs by the door and started dressing in a hurry.

Fay was working the mitten off Stillman's left hand. "I still think you should get out of those cold clothes, Ben," she said. "Let the heat get at you. It won't do you any good to go over to the Hawleys' half-froze."

Stillman gazed at her. He wanted to grab her and kiss her and hold her close, but Durnam and the children were watching. She met his gaze. He could tell she had read his thoughts by the way her eyes crinkled slightly at the corners and by the soft light flashing in each.

"No," he said, shaking his head. "I'll thaw out here in a minute. No telling what could be happening over there."

"You're right," she said, her thoughts returning to the cabin.

"Bad?" Stillman asked her.

He could tell she didn't want to say anything in front of the others. She just nodded her head slightly and tossed his mittens before the fire. He grabbed her hand, gently turning her back to him. "Are you all right?"

She nodded, her eyes downcast. To the girl, she said, "Rose, would you bring the sheriff some tea, please?"

While the girl was getting Stillman's tea, the boy went out and Leon came in, chuffing and sighing and stamping his feet.

"Make that two teas, Rose," Durnam told his daughter.

Durnam pulled a rocker up next to the stove. "Here you go, Deputy, have ya a seat."

"Don't mind if I do," Leon said, untying his scarf and removing his hat. He walked stiffly over to the chair, turned around, placed both hands on the arms, and eased himself down with a slow sigh. "I don't believe I was ever this cold durin' the Army . . . an' I tell ya, those barracks at Fort Assin'boine . . . they was chilly!"

Fay took his hat and set it on the floor before the fire. "Oh, you men are froze," she complained. "Take off your gloves," she ordered Leon.

He shook his head. "I don't think I'll be able to get 'em back on again. How are you, anyway?"

"Better than you at the moment. Please take your gloves off so I can warm them for you."

Leon looked at Ben, who shrugged ironically. "Better do as you're told, partner. There's no arguing with that woman."

While they drank their tea, Stillman questioned Fay about the state of the Hawley cabin at the time she'd escaped.

"Adler," Stillman mused, sipping his second cup of tea. "I arrested an Adler years back. Kind of fits the description of this fella, but he'd be older by now."

"Could be family," Leon said.

"Not a very nice family," Fay said. "You two be careful."

"I'll cover his if he covers mine," Leon said, regarding Stillman ironically.

Stillman finished his tea, gave his cup to Fay, and worked his way out of his chair. He stood, taking inventory of his nerve endings, finding that his feet, while still a little sore in places, were solidly beneath him and no longer feeling like cinder blocks. He turned to the boy, who'd returned from the barn and was hanging up his cold-weather clothes on the peg behind the door.

"The horses ready, son?"

"All ready, Sheriff."

"You ready?" Stillman asked his deputy.

"I reckon as ready as I'll ever be."

Stillman turned to Fay, who stood before him, gazing up at him, her lustrous brown eyes large with worry. With her hair down and mussed, she looked as attractive as he'd ever seen her. What he wouldn't give to be with her alone right now, and for everyone at the Hawley cabin to be safe and sound in their beds . . . for Jody and Crystal to be safe and out of this storm.

"We'll be careful," he assured her. Taking her delicate face gently in his big hands, he leaned down and kissed her lips.

"You'd better," she said, placing her hands on his and wrinkling her lovely brows.

Durnam cleared his throat and stood up from his chair at the kitchen table. He swallowed, his eyes turning grave. "Sheriff, I'd like to help—"

"Don't even think about it, Mr. Durnam," Stillman said. "I could certainly use your assistance, but you're needed here with your children."

Durnam looked vaguely relieved as he turned to the little blond girl, Rose, staring up at him with concern. He cupped her chin in his hand, nodding.

Stillman pulled on his gloves and donned his hat, tying the earflaps down tight beneath his chin. He met Leon at the door. "We'll be back in a few hours," he told Fay. "Whatever you do . . . no matter how long we're gone . . . you stay put and don't open this door for anyone." He turned to Durnam. "They could get around us, so keep your guns close."

"I will," Durnam said, glancing at the revolver on the table.

Stillman turned and opened the door. Fay grabbed him, kissed him once more, and let him go.

20

SOMETHING THUMPED. WAYNE Adler opened his eyes with a start. "What was that?"

Benji, on the chair facing the sitting room, turned to him. "Just a log in the stove."

Adler grumbled and smacked his lips together, looking around the sitting room, where Mama still sat beside her wounded half-breed, the two Hawley women sat holding each other like the world was on fire, and ol' Earl dozed, bent uncomfortably forward in his chair, like he was trying to puzzle out a crack in the puncheon floor.

Adler was sitting at the kitchen table, kicked back in his chair, arms crossed over his chest. The makeshift bandage he'd wrapped around his head was dark with dry blood. The bleeding had stopped and the wound wasn't throbbing as badly. He felt better after the half-hour nap, not as tired and anxious.

He'd made Benji sleep first, while Wayne had watched the hostages. Then he'd woken Benji, ordered him to keep his eyes peeled and his gun out, while he himself took a snooze in his chair. Neither of them had slept for over twenty-four hours, and Adler knew they'd need sleep for whatever the hell they were going to do come morning or when the storm quit.

Adler looked at the clock over the settee. Five-thirty. "No sign of ol' Tony, eh?" he asked Benji.

"No sign of him, Wayne," Benji said, his gun in his hand aimed at the sitting room, a worried look on his face.

Adler got up and stretched, walked to the stove, and poured himself a fresh cup of coffee. He strode to a window and looked out. The wind had nearly died and the eastern sky was softening. The storm was apparently over, but there was a good seven or eight inches of snow on the ground, blown into four-foot drifts and higher. It would have been best to wait here until it melted off. Getting horses through that, all the way to Canada, would be one hell of a chore. At the rate they'd have to travel, it would take them a week just to make the border. Another week to make Medicine Hat.

Waiting here for at least another day or two, until the next chinook, would have been an option if that goddamn Riemersma had come back and said he'd caught up to the teacher and cut her throat. But he hadn't, and it looked like he wouldn't. Which meant he and the teacher had either frozen to death, or the teacher had gotten away and ol' Tony had bought a bullet over at the Durnam outfit.

That, in turn, meant others knew that Adler and Phelps were here in the Hawley cabin, and could very well be on the way here right now . . . even as Adler stood blinking his sleepy eyes, staring thoughtfully out the window, and sipping his coffee.

His heartbeat quickened as the gravity of the situation suddenly found its way to his brain. He imagined cowboys from the Durnam ranch approaching the cabin, horses crunching in the snow, the men armed with Winchesters—five, six, maybe ten seasoned riders. . . . Or maybe someone got to town and warned the teacher's husband, Ben Stillman himself. . . .

Benji got up to stoke the sitting room stove, and the girl whimpered.

"Tell her to shut the fuck up!" Adler shouted at the kid's mother, his nerves suddenly jangled all over again. He felt like a rat trapped in a very small box.

Doreen Hawley gave a start, eyes wide with horror, and held her daughter close, shushing the girl as she stroked her back.

"I got some thinkin' to do an' I can't think if she's gonna keep squealing like a stuck sow ever' time one of us moves!"

"I'm sorry . . . she'll be quiet now," Doreen said.

"See to it she is," Adler grumbled, sitting back down in his chair.

He took his face in both hands and ran the situation through his brain, trying to decide what to do. He figured his chances were good that Tony and the teacher were dead, but that didn't mean he and Benji were safe. Someone would eventually come looking for the teacher, probably Stillman himself.

No, they couldn't just wait here for the snow to melt. It was too risky. They had to ride. But where?

Adler took his hair in his fists and gently pulled. *Where?*

"How far's Big Sandy from here?" he asked no one in particular.

Crystal turned slowly from her husband, her face drawn with worry. The half-breed hadn't been conscious for some time now. "About twelve miles," she said, adding tiredly but with an edge of wry encouragement, "You can make it, Wayne. The storm's over. Go."

Adler smiled in spite of his foul mood. "You'd like that, wouldn't you, bitch?"

"Very much," Crystal said with a droll nod.

Her insolence was infuriating. "Maybe I'll take you into the back room instead, teach you some respect."

"Better be careful," Crystal said glibly. "You know what happened to your friend back there."

Adler's hand went to his gun. It froze there. Better not, he told himself. You might need her later. That thought sparked another.

He stood there staring icily at Crystal and working out a plan that came to him almost of its own accord. They'd leave now, and take Mama with them. They'd leave the mother and daughter alive in the cabin, to inform whoever came that if they followed Adler and Phelps, Mama would die. She'd die the very minute Adler became aware he was being followed.

He and Benji would go to Big Sandy, which Adler knew was on the Great Northern line. They'd take a train south, maybe light out for Mexico instead of Canada, get away from all this snow....

Adler swung his look at Benji, who was very obediently watching the hostages with his gun drawn, just like Adler had told him. The kid was too slow and stupid to take to Mexico. He'd get them caught and hanged for sure. Adler decided he'd kill Benji as soon as they left the farmyard.

That way all the money would be Adler's, and he'd be free to flee on his own. Him and fifty thousand dollars in hard, cold cash . . . in Mexico.

What wouldn't that kind of money buy south of the border?

His heart racing eagerly, relieved to finally have a workable plan, Adler turned to the mother and daughter cowering on the floor by the stove. "Get up," he ordered them.

The mother looked at him, fear building quickly in her eyes.

"I'm not going to kill you—get *up!*"

The mother clutched the daughter. "No . . . please."

"Are you deaf?" Adler barked. "I said I'm not going to kill you. Now get up, or I *will!*"

The mother pushed the daughter off her lap, then climbed awkwardly to her feet, watching Adler with haunted eyes. The girl watched him, too, with eyes even more haunted than her mother's. Earl was watching him now, too, brows furrowed with concern.

Adler walked over to the trapdoor beside the table. "This is a cellar, I take it?" he asked the mother.

She nodded.

Adler bent down and pulled the door up by the ring. The smell of earth and potatoes wafted out of the dark hole. "Get down there."

The mother turned to Earl. He didn't look at her. He was watching Adler, trying to puzzle out the outlaw's motives.

"Get down there—I'm not going to fucking ask you again!" Adler roared, his voice cracking.

The mother took the daughter by the hand and led her to the hole. The mother went first down the steep, shallow stairs. The daughter followed, not taking her eyes off Adler. When they were hidden in the darkness at the bottom of the cellar, Adler said, "When someone comes for us, here's what I want you to tell them. Are you listening?"

No answer.

"I said *are you listening?*"

"Yes," the mother said, voice quavering.

"I want you to tell them that I took Mama, and that

if they follow me, Mama will die. If I so much as just think—if I so much as get the teeny-weeniest suspicion someone's on my trail, Mama here is gonna buy a bullet in her belly. Do you understand?"

The sound of muffled crying came through the hole.

At the end of his patience, Adler rolled his eyes. "Do you understand?"

"Yes," came the thin, tearful reply. "What . . . what about my husband and Jody?"

"That's all you have to remember, Mother," Adler said, letting go of the door, which slammed shut with a roar, making the whole house jump. Dust sifted down from the rafters.

"What are you doing, Wayne?" Crystal asked him. Fear had returned to her eyes, and Adler was happy to see it.

"Shut up," he sneered.

"Wayne." It was Benji. "Wayne . . . you said . . . you said 'I' instead of 'we.' "

Adler turned to him with a look of strained patience, not wanting to answer a bunch of fool questions. He had half a mind to put a bullet in the moron's head right now. "What?"

"You said if *you* was to get the teeny-weeniest . . . I mean . . . if *you* was to think someone was on your trail . . . like you was alone . . . like I wouldn't be with you. . . ." Benji's brow was wrinkled in painful thought. He was vaguely suspicious, while not sure why.

Adler understood. He draped an arm over the big man's shoulders. "Just a manner of speech, Benji, my boy . . . just a manner of speech. I wouldn't go nowhere without you. That just wouldn't be right, would it? Now, didn't I tell you back in the pen that if you broke that fella—what was his name? Grago?—if you broke his knees for me, crippled him good without killin' him, I'd make you rich? Didn't I say that?"

"Well, that's what you said back then, Wayne, but . . ."

"And I meant it, Benji, my friend. Every word of it. I never, and I mean never, went back on a promise." He gave the big idiot a brotherly squeeze. "Besides, how in the hell could I spend all that money by my lonesome? Huh?" He faked a laugh. "How in the hell could I do that? That'd be one hell of a lot of women, an' I ain't that young anymore. Ha-ha-ha!"

Benji's mood lightened. He cracked a grin, which soon became a smile. He rolled his eyes and shrugged his bulky shoulders. "Well . . . I guess . . . I guess I'm sorry, Wayne. I guess I shouldn't o' thought such a thing."

"No you shouldn't have, but hey, you can make it up to me by doin' one thing."

"What's that?"

"You stay in here and keep your eyes on the boys here while I go out and saddle us a couple horses."

"What about her?" Benji said, looking at Crystal.

"She's comin' with me. If anyone's pokin' around out there, I'll have a little bargainin' power."

Crystal snapped her head around. "What!"

Adler regarded her coldly. "You're comin' with me, nice and calmlike. If you raise a fuss, Benji here's gonna put a bullet in both their heads. Understand?"

Crystal just looked at him, awestruck.

"If you raise any kind of a fuss," Adler continued, "I'm gonna signal Benji with one shot to go ahead and kill 'em—your half-breed and good ol' Earl."

Adler looked at Earl. Earl returned the gaze. He was too fatigued to look anything but cowed, just wanting the whole ordeal over, just wanting to stay alive and to feel his hands again, which, tied as tightly as they were, he hadn't felt in hours.

Adler swung back to Crystal. "Understand?" he yelled.

She took a deep breath. Will this night ever end? she wondered. "All right."

Adler gestured at the pegs on either side of the door, from which all shapes and sizes of cold-weather gear hung. "All right, pick yourself out some duds and let's get movin'."

When she'd bundled up, Crystal stepped outside at Adler's command. Adler grabbed the saddlebags containing the loot. "I'll take these now, just so we don't forget," he told Benji with a wink.

He started after Crystal, stopped short, and turned back to the big man staring after him, vaguely suspicious. "Oh, and, in exactly fifteen minutes, kill 'em both . . . quiet-like . . ."

He jerked his head at the hostages, grinned, winked, and went out.

21

THE HORSES THE boy had saddled for Stillman and McMannigle were stout, big-bottomed animals with a lot of wind. They had little problem negotiating the drifts between the Durnam ranch and the Hawley farm. The biggest problem Stillman ran into on the way over, besides the cold, was thinking about how to free the hostages without getting any of them killed.

He'd encountered a similar problem once before, when he was a U.S. deputy marshal. A gang of bank robbers had taken two tellers hostage, and holed up in a shack down by the Big Horn River. Stillman and three other deputies tracked them and waited outside in an aspen grove. When it became clear from the screams that the tellers were about to be killed, Stillman and the other deputies stormed the place.

It had been a messy business. Two of the five outlaws and one deputy were killed, another deputy was wounded, and one of the hostages took a ricochet through the abdomen. He and the other hostage survived, but it had been sheer luck that had saved them.

In situations like this, Stillman knew that luck was the

biggest player of all, and you just had to hope she played on your side of the table. If she didn't, Stillman could very well lose two young people he'd come to love like his very own, and an innocent family would die.

"How do you wanna play this?" Leon asked him as they hunkered down behind a box elder, about seventy yards north of the house. They'd picketed their horses well back in a ravine, far enough away that no nickers or snorts could be heard inside the cabin.

Clutching his Henry rifle before him, Stillman stared at the house. He had a view of the north side, where there were two windows, one in front, one in back. The front window shone with flickering lantern light that bled a thin sheen onto the cordwood stacked against the house. Behind the house was a privy. Before it, to Stillman's right, were the barn, stable, well house, and corrals.

Stillman took a deep breath. "Well, there's only two of them, so it shouldn't be too terribly hard."

Leon chuckled without mirth and gave his head a shake. "Where have I heard that before?"

"Yeah, well, I guess I'm just trying to look on the bright side. The main thing is, we have to make sure none of the others get shot."

"I hear that."

"And," Stillman added, sliding his gaze to the deputy, "if you shoot, shoot to kill. We don't want either of those two bastards taking one of the hostages with them when they go."

Leon nodded. "I hear that, too."

"Fay said there was a back door. Why don't you sneak around behind the privy and approach from that angle? I'll try to get onto the porch without anyone hearing me, and go in the front." Stillman turned to Leon again, tugged on his arm. "If either one of those two bastards has a gun in his hand, shoot him. Even if he's not aiming the damn thing. No questions asked."

"Better safe than sorry," Leon agreed.

"I'll give you ten minutes to get situated, then I'm going in," Stillman said.

McMannigle nodded, slid a cautious glance at the house, then headed north through the thinly scattered trees, abandoned field implements, and wagon parts poking out of the snow. He hadn't been gone a minute, however, before the front door scraped open and muffled voices carried on the lessening wind.

Stillman tossed a northward glance, instantly wishing he could stop Leon. If someone was leaving the cabin, their plans might have to change. But Leon was long gone. There was little chance he would have heard the door above the wind.

Crouching, Stillman crept to his right, wanting a better view of the porch. He came to another tree and slid a look around the trunk. In the darkness before the cabin he saw two people head across the yard toward the barn. The two remaining outlaws? Only if everyone inside was either tied . . . or dead. The latter possibility knocked Stillman's ribs together with a shudder, and his heart quickened its beating, drumming against his sternum.

Goddamn . . .

He thought about following the two to the barn, but decided against it. First, he had to have a look inside the cabin. He had to know who was in there and who wasn't. No matter what had just transpired, there was either one gunman in the cabin, or none at all. If there was one, Stillman and McMannigle would take him first, then go after the other man in the barn.

Gripping the Henry in his mittened hands, he inspected the windows carefully. Seeing no silhouettes, he made a dash and leapt behind the wood pile, his breathing hard and raspy, the cold expanding in his lungs and making his chest ache. He carefully lifted his head and peered in the window. Before him lay the kitchen and a table covered with an oilcloth and a mess of empty bottles, tin cups, plates, an overflowing ashtray, and playing cards.

There were several lanterns situated in various parts of the cabin, casting as many shadows as thin, buttery light. He could make out several figures in the sitting room, the most prominent of which was a giant of a man, the top of his head nearly scraping the rafters. He stood beside a man hunched in a chair. Earl? Stillman couldn't tell. What he could tell, however, was that the standing man's arms hung stiffly at his sides. It was a threatening stance if Stillman had ever seen one.

He sensed the danger, but before he'd started toward the porch, he saw the big, standing man's hands come up over his head, come together, then jerk suddenly down against the back of the sitting man's head.

"Ahhh!" Stillman heard the cry through the window. It was followed by a crash, like that of a chair falling.

Stillman was on the porch in three quick strides. He punched the latch and threw the door open just as the big man delivered a vicious kick—it was more of a thrust, really, the sole of his boot facing out—to the knee of the man on the floor.

Stillman had torn off his right mitten before he'd reached the porch. Lifting the Henry and jacking a shell in the breech, he placed a finger on the trigger, giving a tentative squeeze.

"Freeze!"

The big man turned toward Stillman, the bizarre grin on his face becoming a child's expression of utter bewilderment. "Who-who are you?"

"Sheriff," Stillman announced, just as Leon thundered

through the back door, his Spencer out before him. "Lift that weapon out of your holster real slow, with your left hand, and set it on the floor."

Earl rolled on the floor, groaning painfully, his hands still tied to the overturned chair.

"Wayne . . . Wayne ain't gonna like this," the big man blubbered. "I . . . I ain't goin' back to no pen . . . they don't treat me right. . . ."

"I bet they don't," Stillman said. "Just the same, drop that gun."

The big man stared at Stillman and Leon, who stood to each side of the man, rifles aimed.

A belligerent light grew in the man's eyes, and he trained it on Stillman. "I ain't goin' back to no pen . . . they don't treat me nice . . . !"

"Watch it, Ben! Watch it!" Leon warned.

"I ain't goin' back to no pen!" the big man cried, balling his fists at his sides, rolling his enormous shoulders, and moving steadily toward Stillman.

"Stop or I'll shoot!" Stillman ordered, not wanting to shoot the man, whose gun was still in his holster.

The big man brought back a roast-sized fist and propelled it forward in what could have been a devastating roundhouse. Stillman ducked. The fist arced over his head, making the air whistle. Coming back up, Stillman poked the butt of his rifle into the big man's gut. The big man's lungs expelled a thunderous sigh. Not all the air had left his lips before Stillman poked his rifle butt against the man's face, breaking his nose.

The man took two steps back, his eyes rolling around, an outraged expression on his face. "I . . ." he wailed. "I'm gonna break your knees!"

But before he'd moved another muscle, Stillman off-cocked the Henry and swung the rifle around like a club, connecting soundly with the right side of the big man's head. There was the sound of heavy bones cracking and skin breaking. The man sank to his knees, the light leaving his eyes. Then he fell over sideways and lay still. Stillman hadn't wanted to kill him, but he knew the man was dead, his skull crushed.

Stillman turned his attention to the hostages—Jody lying on the settee, lifting his head and eyeing Stillman groggily, Earl rolling on the floor and groaning in pain. "I think he broke my knee," the farmer moaned.

"Where are the others?" Stillman asked.

"My wife and daughter's in the cellar," Earl said through gritted teeth. "Adler's got Crystal in the barn. I hope you kill that son of a bitch."

While Leon removed his knife from his scabbard and went to work on Earl's tethers, Stillman followed Earl's glance to the cellar door, bent down, and yanked on the ring. The door came up and fell down flat against the floor with a boom. "You're safe now, Mrs. Hawley . . . Candace. Come on up."

The two came up the steps slowly, blinking their eyes against the light. They looked like they'd been down there for twenty years. Seeing they were all right physically, Stillman made a beeline for Jody.

"No," Jody protested, shaking his head as though it weighed twenty pounds. "Crystal . . . he's . . . Adler's got her in the barn. He's gonna light a shuck!"

Stillman shoved the lad back down on the settee. "Easy, son, easy." He removed the makeshift bandage Crystal had placed over the wound. It was sopping wet with blood. Stillman made a face.

Jody grabbed his wrist and squeezed with what little strength he had. "I'm okay . . . *Crystal* . . . !"

His face was blanched and soaking with sweat, and his teeth were chattering. Stillman knew he wasn't okay, but first he had to see to Crystal. He snugged the afghan about Jody's chest, walked to the door, and closed it. He turned to Leon, who was kneeling down by Earl, examining the man's knee. Mrs. Hawley and Candace were there, as well, gazing at their husband and father, shocked to be alive.

"Adler's in the barn," Stillman said, moving to a window and stealing a glance across the barnyard. The dark was softening, shapes solidifying against the sky. He wondered if Adler had already left the barn on a horse, having heard the commotion in the cabin.

He looked at Leon, who was gingerly squeezing Earl's knee.

"How's the leg?" Stillman asked him.

Leon shook his head. "I don't think it's broken, but it sure is bruised."

"Oh, Earl, poor Earl," Doreen was cooing, smoothing her husband's hair against his head. Candace just stared at the knee, which Leon had exposed when he'd cut the man's pants with his knife. Her expression was glassy-eyed, stony. Stillman wondered if she'd ever get over what she'd witnessed here.

"You stay with these people," he told Leon, heading for the door to the back hall. "I'm going out to the barn."

"Wait," Leon protested, gaining his feet. "You can't go out there alone."

Stillman turned. He'd opened the door, and his right hand was on the outside knob. "I have to. You need to be here in case the bastard comes back while I'm circling the barn."

Leon thought about it, not liking it, and nodded. He sighed, knowing it was the only way.

Stillman disappeared down the hall.

22

CRYSTAL KNEW THAT if she went with Adler, she and her baby would die. She could not withstand a ride on the back of a horse in any kind of weather, least of all bone-splitting cold and snow so deep the horse would have to lunge. Common sense told her that, and so did the sharp pains that had been shooting through her belly for the past ninety minutes, making her deathly afraid she was about to go into labor.

As she stood in the barn alley, in the foggy light shed by a bull's-eye lamp hanging from a nail, she watched Adler saddle a horse, and tried desperately to come up with a solution to her dilemma. She knew one thing for certain. She could not get on that horse.

But what would happen if she refused? He'd probably force her into the saddle and tie her there, or kill her outright and replace her with either Candace or her mother. She had to attack the son of a bitch. That was the only way. But what, in her condition, could she do?

She looked around, squinting her eyes at the shadows beyond the dim sphere of lantern light. She thought she could make out several wooden handles lined against the

wall. No doubt one of those handles belonged to a pitchfork. If she could just slip over there without Adler seeing her . . .

She'd have to wait until he'd started saddling the second horse. That would put the already saddled horse
between her and the outlaw, shielding her from view.

Grimly, Adler tightened the belly strap on the first
horse, then walked around behind the horse to the other,
tied to a post about ten yards away from Crystal. "You
just stay right there, Mama," he told her, as if reading
her mind. "I'll have this black saddled and we'll be out
of here in just a minute." He chuckled to himself and
grabbed the second saddle off a stall partition.

As soon as he gave his back to Crystal, Crystal started
moving sideways, one step at a time, toward the tools
along the wall, hoping against hope at least one of them
was a pitchfork or an ax. She breathed quietly, careful
not to make any noise as her booted feet stepped down
on the straw-covered floor. When she finally made it
beyond the lantern light, she quickened her steps
slightly, her heart starting to pound with anticipation.

As she neared the wall, she gave her back to Adler
and studied the tools. There were several ax handles, a
couple of scythes . . . and a pitchfork. She reached for it,
wrapped one mittened hand around the splintered handle, and turned with it toward Adler. She hurried into
the light just as Adler turned from the saddle.

"Just stay right there, Mama," he said lazily, then gave
a grunt as he tightened the belly strap. He said to the
horse, "Come on, you bastard. Let out your breath, damn
you."

When the strap was cinched, he retrieved his saddlebags from the stall partition and turned toward Crystal,
who held the pitchfork behind her back, trying to appear
as casual as she could. She tried to ignore the stabs of

pain shooting through her midsection. As soon as the bastard's back was to her again, she'd stab him with the pitchfork—give him all four tines good and deep in his back.

He approached her with the saddlebags, grinning. He gave her a lascivious wink and threw the saddlebags over the back of the first horse he'd saddled. "Whatcha gonna do with that, Mama?" he asked lightly.

Crystal's heart did a somersault. "What?"

"That pitchfork you got from the wall yonder. What you gonna do . . . clean the barn?" Adler laughed, still giving her his back, daring her.

"You son of a bitch!" she screamed, bringing the pitchfork around, lifting it awkwardly, and lunging forward with the tines pointed toward Adler.

He swung around to face her, stepped sideways, and slapped the pitchfork away. Crystal half-screamed and half-cried with utter dejection. Lacking the strength for another attack, she dropped the pitchfork, and sank to her knees, feeling the tears wash over her face as she cried. All hope was gone. She and her baby and Jody . . . they all would die.

"Now I ain't got time for no more foolin' around, Mama!" Adler barked. "Get your ass on that horse over there . . . we're gettin' the hell outta here!"

Crying, Crystal shook her head. Let him kill her now. She was not getting on the horse. She was not doing anything else this madman told her to do. "No," she said. "No, no, no!"

"Goddamnit!" Adler bawled, grabbing the iron off his hip and aiming at her. "I said get up!"

He froze, as if suddenly possessed, and jerked a look toward the back of the barn. Crystal watched him through her tears, vaguely curious.

"Who's there?" Adler yelled.

He didn't wait for an answer. He lunged toward Crystal, grabbed her arm, and jerked her to her feet. He swung her around in front of him, gripping her tightly with one hand while holding his gun with the other.

"I've gotta girl here in the family way!" he shouted. "She's gonna die if you don't come out where I can see you."

"All right, all right," a voice called from the shadows. "I'm coming out. Take it easy."

"You take it easy," Adler called. "Get out here, or this girl dies."

As Adler gripped Crystal's arm so tightly that pain shot through her shoulder, she watched a tall, rugged-looking man in a buckskin mackinaw and fur hat step out of the darkness. He held a rifle out away from his body, in a gesture of acquiescence.

"Ben!" Crystal exclaimed.

Stillman ignored her. His eyes were on the outlaw. "Here I am. Now just take it easy."

"Stillman," Adler breathed. "That really you?"

Stillman didn't say anything.

Adler paused. Crystal felt him shake, and realized he was laughing. "It's the great Ben Stillman. You put my brother away, you bastard."

"In the flesh," Stillman said, his eyes straying quickly from Adler to Crystal, then back again. "Why don't you let the girl go? I'll be your hostage. No one will come after you if I tell them not to."

"No one will come after me if I have Mama here, either. That means I can kill the great Stillman right now!"

Adler aimed the gun at Stillman, who dove to one side as the gun exploded. The bullet tore into a joist with a thunk. Stillman was twisting around, trying to bring his rifle up, when Adler aimed again. Seeing he didn't have time to bring his rifle to bear, Stillman dropped it and scrambled into a stall. As the gunman fired, Crystal yelled, "No!" and hit the revolver. The slug sailed wild.

"You bitch!" Adler backhanded Crystal, who fell on her back with a scream. Adler leveled his revolver at her, cocking the hammer. "You're dead now, Mama!"

"No!" Stillman shouted as he scurried to his feet, drawing his Colt .44. His ears rang with horror as he saw Adler's gun pointing at Crystal, knowing he wouldn't be able to bring his own weapon to bear on Adler in time to save her. He'd get the gunman, he knew, but not before Adler had shot Crystal. The thought was a clean slap across his face, like a pitiless, polar wind, turning his knees to jelly.

He gave a start as two gun reports, one on top of the other, slammed through the fetid barn. Just before he'd gotten his own .44 aimed at the gunman, he'd seen the gunman jerk as a cloudy substance puffed out from this side of the man's head, a quarter second before Adler's own gun sprouted flames. Stillman's revolver barked as Adler turned toward him, giving him his chest. Stillman's bullet plowed through the man's belly, knocking him back against a stall. He stood there, already dead, head going back, and slumped to the floor like a puppet cut from its strings. He fell lazily over, as if for a nap.

From that angle, Stillman could see that a bullet had torn through his head, leaving a dark, wet hole to which hair clung.

"Jody!" Crystal cried.

Stillman turned to her, amazed she was alive, watching her scramble, half-crawling, toward the shadows beyond the light, realizing that the bullet Adler had fired at her had been nudged wild by the bullet that had torn through his brain. Heart still pounding, his thoughts rac-

ing, Stillman stepped out of the stall into which he'd
thrown himself, and walked toward the front of the barn.

There, at the edge of the light, Crystal was kneeling
beside Jody, who had fallen to one knee, a revolver in
his left hand. Crystal was hugging him and crying and
calling his name. Jody dropped the revolver and put his
good arm around her neck.

He looked up as Stillman approached. He tried a smile,
removed his hand from Crystal's neck, and opened it.
"Left-handed," he said. "I got him left-handed . . . what
do you think of that?" His face was drawn, sweat-beaded,
and pale, but his eyes were alive.

"I think that was some fine shootin', son," Stillman
said.

Crystal struggled out of her husband's grasp. Her
voice was both jubilant and chiding. "Jody . . . what are
you *doing* out here?"

Weakening, he leaned on his hand. "I grabbed that
big fella's gun out of his holster while Leon was tending
Earl, and snuck out the back." His gaze found Crystal
and turned wry. "I wasn't about to let you ride off with
that jasper and his loot."

Stillman heard boots crunching snow. A figure appeared in the partially open front door. It was Leon. He
gazed around silently for a moment, his gun drawn. "Everybody all right?"

"He's dead," Stillman said, waving his gun at Adler.

"I turned around, and the kid here was gone," Leon
said.

Stillman holstered his pistol. "Lucky he was, too, or
Crystal would be dead." He leaned down to help Jody
to his feet. "Can you walk, son? We have to get you
back into the cabin. Looks like you opened up that
wound again."

"I can walk," Jody said weakly.

He tried to stand, but Crystal remained kneeling. "I hate to tell you men this," she said, "but I think my water's broke."

Late that morning, when the sun had come up and a warm chinook wind had turned the top of the new-fallen snow to a glittering-wet crust, and water dripped from the eaves, a sharp crack sounded in the cabin. It was followed by the wails of a newborn baby.

"I do believe it's a boy," Stillman said as he returned to the sitting room, rolling down his sleeves. He and Mrs. Hawley had performed the delivery, while young Candace ran for water and clean towels.

Jody was reclining on the settee, head and back propped up with pillows, covered with a heavy quilt. Leon had cleaned his wound with whiskey and covered it with a salve Earl kept around for doctoring his stock's screwworms and fence cuts. The young man's forehead was still slick with fever, but he was looking better.

"Uh . . . a boy?" he asked Stillman now, trying to sit up.

"Big strapping lad!" Stillman announced with a grin. "Practically a full head of brown hair, blue eyes, and hung like a horse!"

He, Leon, and Earl laughed. Earl was sitting in the kitchen with a snowpack on his knee. Leon was standing before the window, where he'd been restlessly awaiting the news, hands thrust in his pockets of his denim britches.

"Your old man would be right proud of you, boy," Stillman told Jody. "Proud of both you and that woman o' yours."

Jody smiled with pride. A touch of concern entered his gaze. "Crystal? She's—"

"Fit as a fiddle. Tired, though. She's probably asleep by now."

"Been through a lot, that girl."

"You all have," Stillman said, turning to Earl. "Reckon you can put up with the Harmon clan a few more days? Neither the baby nor Crystal should be doing any traveling until at least the end of the week. Neither should Jody."

"Oh, I got stock to feed," Jody protested, pushing himself up.

"Sit back there, boy!" Leon bellowed. "You open that hole again, I'll thump your noggin. I'll take care of your stock until you're well enough to travel back to your ranch. Then I'll pick you and your family up in a wagon."

Jody looked at the black man warmly. Before he could speak, Leon threw up his hands. "Hey, I'm lookin' forward to gettin' out o' town for a while. Those women over to Missus Lee's—I don't think they heard about the 'Mancipation Proclamation. They got me running like a slave!" He grinned.

Jody grinned back. Stillman retrieved his coat and hat from a peg by the door. "Well, I'll be heading out."

"Where you going?" Jody asked him.

"I'm gonna throw the outlaws over their horses and head back to town . . . pick up Fay along the way. While you were sleeping, the temperature rose about thirty degrees." He paused, casting his troubled eyes at Earl. "I'm sorry about all that's happened here. I wish I could've got here sooner."

"Wasn't your fault, Sheriff," the farmer said, shaking his head.

"I hope your women'll be all right. Somethin' like this . . ."

"I know," Earl said, nodding. "It takes some forgetting. I'll do my best to help 'em forget. I have a feelin' that little lad up yonder's doin' as much for them as them for him."

Stillman nodded and smiled, then shrugged into his coat. To Leon, he said, "See you back in town in a few days."

"I'll be there."

To Jody, he said, "You get well, and raise that boy the way your old man raised you."

Jody pursed his lips. "I'll do that, Ben. I sure am glad you got here when you did."

"So am I," Stillman said. He opened the door, flooding the room with bright sunshine, and left.

EPILOGUE

Two weeks later . . .

EARLY IN THE morning of a bright, springlike day, with a warm zephyr drying the last of the mud left from the melted snow, Doc Evans stepped out of his big, red house on the butte overlooking Clantick, clutching a canvas war bag in his right hand, drawing on the stogie clamped in his teeth.

He paused on his back step. The steps themselves and the wood railing were badly in need of paint. Frowning, he turned to the house looming up behind him, silhouetted by the sun lifting in the east. Hell, the whole house could use a fresh coat. And the weeds in the beds, brown and limp from the long winter, could use a good pulling, the soil a turning. In a month or two, he might just hire a kid to come over and do a little work about the place.

Evans did not reflect on the singularity of his reflections, which in itself was singular. There were few men about Clantick more reflective than the doctor. No, he did not wonder that a man like him—a devout slob wedded to sloth—should be suddenly thinking about the appearance of his hovel. Instead, he gave a curt, self-satisfied nod and, still puffing on the stogie, headed for the decidedly run-down stable sitting back in the weeds of his butte-top yard.

The old lady who had owned the place before Evans did had run chickens out of the stable, and the chickens had eaten the grass down to the leather. Thistles had grown up in the bald spots, and now Evans decided, only half-consciously but consciously just the same, that it was time for the thistles to go. Maybe he'd try growing grapes there . . . or raspberries. His mother had always grown raspberries against his family's buggy shed back in New York.

Evans threw open the stable doors with a grunt, and tossed his war bag in the back of the black buckboard wagon, which he used for medical runs as well as a hearse, picking up cadavers here and there about the county. For the wry doctor, it was a persistent source of humor that his part-time job as an undertaker was often more lucrative than his primary profession, for which he'd been schooled at considerable cost to his father, a medical man himself.

When he'd hitched the buckboard to the temperamental black, blaze-faced gelding he called Faustus after his favorite character in classical literature, he climbed atop the wagon, slapped the reins against Faustus's back, and was off, Faustus jerking his neck and biting the bit with characteristic mulishness.

Ten minutes later he pulled up before Jensen's Tonsorial Parlor, a primitive board shack on Third Avenue, its two sashed windows—one on either side of the door—eternally fogged by steam. Smoke gushed from the tin chimney poking out of the tin-covered roof.

Evans set the brake, wrapped the reins around it, reached around for his war bag, and jumped down from the wagon. "Stay, Faustus . . . and don't bite anyone, damnit," he ordered as he strode through the shack's wobbly door.

"Jensen, I'll be needing a bath," he called through the steam, which smelled of sweat, hot iron, and wood smoke.

He walked into the back room, where the proprietor, Jensen, was stoking the stove on which two boilers of water steamed. There were three oak tubs situated along the walls, with nearby benches, coat pegs, and small wall mirrors. The doctor chose a tub, set his war bag on the bench, and started undressing.

Meanwhile, the tall, quiet Jensen limped over with sloshing water buckets, and filled the tub without saying anything or even making eye contact with Evans, who was accustomed to the Swede's stoic demeanor. He guessed the man had a right, his wife and four kids having left him several years ago. He lived in a small log shack behind the bathhouse, and when he wasn't boiling water for baths he was cutting wood in the mountains or drinking beer with his only friend, an old Civil War vet named Hyram Pyle.

Evans grabbed his ivory-handled razor from the war bag, and tested the water in the tub with his big toe. Deeming it hot enough, he stepped in and eased himself down, wincing as the steaming water worked its way up his pinkening body.

"You have any soap besides this lye?" Evans called to the Swede, who'd gone into the front room.

The man poked his head through the door. "Nope."

Evans sighed. "Well, it'll have to do, I guess." He sniffed of the pungent cake, which smelled like lard and candlewax, and shook his head. He soaped his sponge and lathered himself, standing when he got to his legs and loins, not wanting to miss an inch. Finally, he lathered his face, opened the razor, and scraped the whiskers off his cheeks.

When he'd finished scrubbing and shaving, he sat back in the tub and smoked a cigar, which was part of his weekly bathing ritual. He didn't smoke as long as he normally did, however. Instead, he rubbed the glowing ash on the floor, tossed the half-smoked stogie onto the bench, stood, grabbed his towel, and dried himself. Using a small clipper he'd packed in his bag, he trimmed his red mustache in the mirror, taking his time, watching closely for vagrant hairs. When he'd waxed it, curving the ends ever so slightly upward, he removed the clean clothes from the war bag, dressed, and stuffed his dirty clothes in the bag.

Returning the unlit stogie to his mouth, he lifted his war bag and went into the front room, where Jensen was sitting, kicked back in his chair, boots crossed on his primitive board desk, arms folded over his chest. His deep, rumbling snores resounded throughout the room. No wonder his family had left him.

The doctor dropped fifty cents on the desk with a metallic clatter. Jensen gave a start and dropped his feet to the floor, frowning as he opened his eyes. "Sorry to wake you, Jens," said Evans, "but I was wondering if you'd hold onto my bag until I come for it?"

Jensen blinked his eyes as he ran his gaze up and down the doctor, his normally inexpressive face registering surprise. What he saw was the good doctor dressed in a full black suit, complete with white linen shirt, watch chain, and a crisp bowler hat. The suit was obviously an older cut, and Evans must have bought it fifteen or twenty pounds ago—it fit rather snugly across the chest and shoulders, riding up a little on the arms.

Furthermore, it needed a hot pressing, for the shirt and pants bore the marks of the storage drawer and war bag.

But all in all, it was a right smart outfit, and the doctor looked at least as dapper as your average whiskey drummer. He smelled like a barbershop.

The stoic Swede did not voice his observations, however. He merely grabbed the bag, said, "Yah, okay," and set the bag on the floor behind his chair.

Evans tipped his hat, went out, unhitched Faustus from the rack, and climbed aboard the stout black wagon. To several of the townsmen sweeping the boardwalks in front of their stores or loafing on the benches as Evans cantered past, the doctor resembled a preacher or the Grim Reaper, dressed as he was in a black suit and driving the black wagon. Like Jensen, none of them articulated their observations beyond a long, curious gaze, a quick shake of the head, and a muttered "Well . . . what do you make of that?"

At the eastern edge of town, Evans turned the wagon south, rode for a block, and pulled up before a neat white house sitting behind a well-kept picket fence, a leafless cottonwood standing tall in the backyard. He set the brake, wrapped the reins around it, removed the stogie from his mouth, and shoved it down in the breast pocket of his suit coat. Then he looked at the house warily, sighed deeply, and climbed down from the wagon.

"Stay, Faustus."

He tripped the latch on the picket gate and walked along the neatly laid cobbles to the front door. He stepped across the narrow porch, opened the screen, and knocked.

He listened. Soft footfalls. A floorboard creaked. The door opened. He tensed.

"Clyde?"

He grabbed the hat off his head.

"Yes . . . uh . . . hello."

Not saying anything, Katherine Kemmet inclined her head and squinted her eyes suspiciously. He hadn't seen her since that fateful night when he'd kissed her and pawed her out at the Nelson ranch. He'd heard she'd delivered another baby since then, but he hadn't heard the news from her. The sun poked through a cloud behind him, and she raised a hand to shield the light from her eyes.

He hesitated. He hadn't expected this to be easy, and it wasn't.

"Well, I just wanted you to know . . . I wanted to say . . ."

He wasn't sure how to finish the sentence. He didn't think he'd ever apologized to a woman before. For some reason, it had never seemed necessary to apologize to the whores he'd frequented, but he felt it necessary to apologize to Katherine. He wasn't sure why. He just knew that, since that night out at the Nelson place, the last time he'd seen her, he'd become aware of a nagging loneliness eating away at his life.

His face was hot. Perspiration trickled under his arms.

He sighed. "I just wanted to know if you'd . . . like to take a ride with me in my wagon and . . . maybe get a bite to eat over at The Boston later . . . you know . . . for lunch . . ."

She inclined her head the other way, cautious. "Why should I?"

It took him several seconds to decide how to answer that. He shrugged and heaved another sigh. "I was just . . . I was just hoping you would." He paused, studied his hat, suddenly feeling the snugness of the suit. "I promise not to try anything like I tried that night. I'm . . . I'm sorry about that. I know it was an unforgivable way for a grown man to act."

She didn't say anything. The breeze played at her hair.

He looked at her. "I don't know what got into me." He swallowed, still feeling awkward but lighter somehow. "Maybe I've been alone too long."

She crossed her arms over her chest, holding the screen open with her foot. "And you drink too much."

His eyes narrowed angrily, his jaw tightening. Then he dropped his chin again, chagrined, and pursed his lips. "Yes, I suppose I do."

"I won't mention that you frequent fallen women."

"Thank you."

"And—" She stopped herself. "Well, I guess that's enough for now." Her voice rose a little, lost some of its edge. She looked him over, a humorous light entering her eyes. "You're all gussied up."

He flushed, embarrassed, flinging his arms stiffly out from his sides. "I just found this in an old trunk up in the attic. My other suit was a little worn, so . . ."

"Why, Clyde," she said, with genuine amusement, "you look almost civilized this morning. In fact, I do believe you shaved!" She laughed.

He sighed once more, staring at the painted porch floor. "Well, I guess I deserve this belittlement. I just wish you'd tell me if it's all for nothing."

"A ride in your lovely wagon, huh?" she said, smirking and sliding her gaze to the black buckboard hitched to Faustus, who stood fidgeting the bit in his mouth. "How could any woman possibly refuse that?" She chuckled. "Let me get my coat and hat."

She started away, turned back, and opened the screen door. Grabbing his face in both her hands, she smiled into his eyes. "It might be too early to tell, but there just might be hope for you yet, Dr. Evans." She pecked him on the cheek, then turned and disappeared inside.

Evans stood facing the screen, surprised. Slowly, he turned back toward the wagon, the breeze lifting his necktie. He stuffed his hands in his pockets, chewed his mustache, and shrugged. A warm light entered his eyes.

Born and raised in North Dakota, Peter Brandvold now lives in Minnesota and Arizona. His email address is brand@prtel.com.

PETER BRANDVOLD